PARALLEL PARKING

a **DATING GAME** novel by Natalie Standiford

LITTLE, BROWN AND COMPANY

New York ⁊ Boston

First Edition: October 2006

Little, Brown and Company
Hachette Book Group USA
1271 Avenue of the Americas, New York, NY 10020
Visit our Web site at www.lb-teens.com

Interior created and produced by Parachute Publishing, L.L.C.
156 Fifth Avenue
New York, NY 10010

ISBN-10: 0-316-11531-2
ISBN-13: 978-0-316-11531-5
LCCN: 2006927909

10 9 8 7 6 5 4 3 2 1

CWO

For John, Jim, Sam, Willard,
and Dad, who taught me to drive a stick shift.

1 Autumn in the Spring

To:	hollygolitely
From:	your daily horoscope

HERE IS TODAY'S HOROSCOPE: CAPRICORN: Open your mouth and close your eyes, and you will get a big surprise. . . .

W elcome! Happy birthday to me!" Autumn squealed.

"Happy Sweet Sixteen, Autumn," Holly Anderson said, dodging a balloon.

Autumn Nelson had transformed the ballroom of the Carlton Bay Country Club into a shrine to herself. A rock band was setting up on a stage in the back of the room while a DJ spun tunes in a corner. Also onstage were two giant blown-up photos of the glory that was Autumn, past and present: a baby picture and a recent glamour shot, with full makeup and long brown hair blown back by a fan. Each table was adorned with a large photo of Autumn at a different age.

"Let's see . . . " Autumn led Holly and her two best friends, Lina Ozu and Madison Markowitz, to their assigned seats. "You're all together at table six—which you can recognize by this adorable picture of me at age six, missing my front teeth. Is that not the cutest?"

Holly looked at the picture and shuddered. Hair in braids, nose covered with freckles, mouth gaping wide to show off the missing teeth, Autumn looked like Dorothy from the Wizard of Oz . . . as a vampire.

Two thin, lanky boys, Walker Moore and Stephen Costello, joined them at the table. Walker, with spiky brown hair and an easygoing smile, was Lina's boyfriend. Stephen, pale and serious, was Mads'.

"This party wins 'Most Self-Indulgent Sweet Sixteen of the Year,'" Stephen said. "So far."

"We've got a long way to go," Holly said. "Lina and Mads turn sixteen this summer."

"This bash will be hard to top," Walker said. He lay the giant photo of Autumn, age six, facedown on the table. "I can't eat with that thing staring at me."

"My parents can't afford anything like this," Mads said.

"And mine would rather die than be so splashy," Lina said.

Autumn climbed up onto the stage and took over the mike. "Hi, everybody! Thanks for coming to my party. Please sit at your assigned table, and don't switch around! I hate it when people do that. The band had this great idea, where every guest can come up and sing a song dedicated to me, if you feel like it. They can play practically any request, so don't be shy! And don't try to slip out into the parking lot to sneak smokes or drinks, because Chloe will be out there for half the party—my dad's trying to get her to cut down on smoking, so she has to do it behind his back. And if she sees you, she'll probably tell on you, because that's the kind of person she is. Just thought I'd warn you. More later!"

She left the stage. Holly glanced at Autumn's father and his girlfriend, Chloe. Chloe, red-faced, yammered something into Mr. Nelson's ear. He put an arm around Chloe, trying to comfort her. Autumn regularly ranted about her in her blog, Nuclear Autumn.

The band played a rocked-out version of "Autumn in New York." They were already pushing the Autumn theme a little hard. Stephen and Mads danced. Holly, Lina, and Walker drank ginger ales and ate crab balls and shrimp cocktail. The sixth person assigned to their table was

Holly's locker neighbor, Sebastiano Altman-Peck.

"I'm going up there," Sebastiano said. "I've got a special song I want to sing to the birthday girl."

"What is it?" Holly asked.

"You'll see." Sebastiano got up on stage and spoke to the band's lead guitarist. "Okay, Autumn," he said, taking the microphone. "This is for you. Happy birthday!"

The band burst into "American Idiot." Sebastiano belted it out. Holly looked to see if Autumn was offended, but she laughed and took it as a joke.

"Sebastiano's pretty good," Lina said.

Mads tugged on Stephen's sleeve. "Let's go up and sing a duet. How about, 'You're the One That I Want'?"

"Uh, nah." Stephen looked uncomfortable. "You go up and sing. You don't need me."

"Sure, I do," Mads said. "Come on."

Stephen shook his head.

"Why not, Stephen?" Holly said. "You can't be any worse than Ingrid, and she's up next."

"I can't sing in front of people," Stephen said. "It's physically painful for me."

"Really?" Holly said. "Physically painful?"

He nodded. "Please don't try to make me, because I won't."

"I'll let you off the hook this time," Mads said. "But

you can't stay this way the rest of your life. Singing is fun!" She stood up. "I think I'll do something from *Grease*," she said.

Up on the stage Ingrid finished singing "And I Love You So." A tall, lean guy with shaggy blond hair took her place at the mike. He wore a tie knotted over a T-shirt, punk rock style, and black sunglasses. A hush fell over the room. It was Sean Benedetto.

Mads sat down. "I'll sing later," she said.

Mads, as Holly knew, had a wicked crush on Sean. Stephen or no Stephen.

Sean sang an old Aerosmith song, "Dream On." His voice wasn't that great, but his stage presence was stunning. Unlike most of the other kids, he had no self-consciousness whatsoever. He sang full throttle but held back just enough to maintain a sense of mystery, to leave the listeners wondering what was on his mind. He rocked his hips, keeping the mike close to his lips. The girls in the audience swooned and screamed as if he were a real rock star. And Holly had to admit, watching him onstage, that he could be a rock star.

She'd always considered Sean a little silly and kind of full of himself. She never quite got why Mads was so obsessed with him. But now, seeing him sing, she had an inkling. She couldn't help swooning a little bit herself.

She glanced at Mads, who looked as if she were in a trance. Her shining eyes followed Sean's every thrust and spin. Holly felt sorry for Stephen, who sat beside Mads, good-naturedly bopping along with the song. Every once in a while he looked at Mads, who seemed to have forgotten he existed. Then he looked away, as if he wanted to pretend that whatever it was he saw in her face wasn't there.

Sean left the stage and was immediately mobbed by girls. Holly didn't see his girlfriend, Jane Cotham, among them. In fact, Jane wasn't anywhere in the room.

The band took a break, the DJ came on duty, and Mads pulled Stephen onto the dance floor as if nothing had happened. Maybe that was why Stephen was so cool about Mads' obvious crush on Sean. Either he didn't notice it, or he did, but realized that it didn't affect her feelings for him or get in the way of their relationship. It was like a movie star crush, totally unrealistic.

Holly danced with Sebastiano, which made her thirsty, so she went to the bar for a glass of water. Sean came up beside her and ordered a beer, which the bartender refused to give him. Sean took it in stride and changed his order to Red Bull.

"Want to step outside for a smoke?" Sean asked Holly. "That chick Chloe is busy choking down shrimp, so the coast is clear."

"I don't smoke," Holly said.

"Me neither," Sean said. "At least, not very often. But I feel like stepping outside anyway."

Holly shrugged. "Okay. Some fresh air would be nice."

Sean pushed open a door marked EMERGENCY EXIT. Holly braced herself for the blare of a fire alarm, but it didn't come. They found themselves in the club parking lot, surrounded by fancy cars.

"So where's your girlfriend?" Holly asked.

"We broke up," Sean said. "It was getting to be a real drag, you know?"

"Who dumped who?" Holly asked. She knew it was none of her business, but something about Sean made her bold—and she was pretty bold to start with.

"Hey, who do you think you're talking to?" Sean asked.

Holly just grinned and shrugged.

"All right, she dumped me," Sean said. "Don't tell anybody."

Holly laughed. "I won't. Why did she dump you?"

"Who knows? She said it was because I was too young for her. That didn't bother her two months ago. I think she likes some other dude. That's cool. It happens. Good luck, whatever."

Holly remembered Mads telling her that she'd seen Jane kiss another guy more than once. So Sean's theory was probably right. Her heart went out to him. Jane must have hurt him, but he was trying to cover it up.

"Is that your Bug?" Sean nodded at Holly's yellow Volkswagen Beetle across the parking lot.

"Yeah," Holly said. "How did you know?"

"I've seen it around school. And it's got a Rosewood parking sticker on it. And you look like the Bug type."

"Really? What type is that?"

"Usually a girl," Sean said. "They go for those 'cute' cars in pretty colors. But also kind of funky and not stuck on status and all that bull. Plus there's that built-in vase with the flower on the dashboard. That's pretty femme."

"Somebody stole my flower," Holly said. "I loved that purple daisy."

"Really? That's not cool."

"I made the mistake of leaving my car unlocked at school," Holly said. "I didn't know an RSAGEr would stoop so low."

"Now you know," Sean said. "They're just as wack as anybody else. Now me, I drive a Jeep. Black." He pointed to it. "What do you think that says about me?"

"Definitely masculine," Holly said. "Simple, functional, yet fun. Ready for action. Up for anything."

"That's me," Sean said. "On the nose." He tapped his nose, then hers. His fingertip was warm and fleshy. "Did you see what Autumn's dad gave her for her birthday?"

"How could I miss it?" Autumn's birthday present was parked in the club driveway—a BMW convertible with a big red bow on top. "What do you think that says about her? Or her dad?"

"That he's got money and he wants everybody to know it," Sean said. "And he'd rather give Autumn stuff than pay attention to her. Not that I don't sympathize. The girl can talk forever, and maybe one percent of what she says is interesting."

Holly laughed again.

"And if Autumn likes her ride, it says she's a showoff and likes attention," Sean said.

"Which we already knew," Holly said.

"Sure, but now other people will know it, too," Sean said. "I'm really into cars. Maybe you can tell. I think they're like a language. Someone should make up a philosophy or something, like, The Benedetto Theory of Cars, where the whole world is described in car terms. I think I'd get the Nobel Prize."

"Or at least a People's Choice Award," Holly said.

"Go ahead, make fun of me. I can handle anything you throw my way."

"I believe it," Holly said.

"Had enough fresh air?" he asked.

"We should probably go back inside," Holly said.

He reached out to open the emergency exit door, but it was locked from the inside. "Guess we've got to go around to the front," he said to Holly.

When they returned to the ballroom, everyone was dancing. Sean led her to the dance floor.

"Come on, let's see how a VW driver moves," he said.

They danced for one song, and then dinner was served. Holly went back to her table.

"Dancing with Sean—how'd that happen?" Lina whispered to her.

"Did Mads notice?" Holly asked.

"She was in the bathroom with me," Lina said. "I walked back in here first, saw you two on the dance floor, and turned Mads around, saying she had crab in her teeth."

Holly thought it was a little silly that Mads had to be protected from seeing her dance with Sean. It was just a dance. It didn't mean anything.

Still, for the rest of the night Holly found herself catching Sean's eye from across the room. They didn't dance together again or say anything to each other. But whenever she looked at him, he was looking at her.

Toward the end of the evening Autumn lost patience with dancing and the band and sat down to tear open her presents.

"Let's get out of here," Holly said to Sebastiano. "Do you need a ride?" Walker and Stephen were taking Lina and Mads home, so Holly would be driving home by herself.

"Sure," Sebastiano said. "Let me just say good-bye to a few people."

"Okay," Holly said. "I'll meet you out by the car." She said good-bye to Mads and Lina and Autumn, who was so busy shredding metallic paper, she barely looked up. Holly went outside and found Sean leaning against her car.

"Heading home?" he said.

"Yep," Holly said. She put her key into the door.

Sean took her by the elbow. "Hey," he said. "I really like you."

Startled, she turned toward him and looked up. He kissed her.

When she'd recovered, Holly glanced around. Did anyone see that? Did Mads? People all around were getting into their cars, but no one seemed to have noticed Sean and Holly.

"What are you doing tomorrow night?" Sean asked.

Holly couldn't remember if she had plans or not. "I don't know. . . ."

"Want to go do something?" he asked.

She needed a moment to take this in. Was Sean Benedetto asking her out? It looked that way. After talking to him that night, she liked him more than she'd thought she would. And she was curious to find out more about him.

But Mads' face loomed in her mind. What would she think if Holly went out with Sean, her eternal crush, her personal rock star? Would she be upset? Holly wasn't sure, but she really loved Mads and wouldn't do anything to hurt her. That overrode any curiosity she had about Sean.

"Sorry, I can't," she told him. "But thanks."

"No problem," Sean said. "See you around."

She watched him walk to his Jeep. Then she got into her car, started it up, and waited for Sebastiano to come find her.

I just kissed Sean, she thought over and over again. *Or, rather, he kissed me.* She had to admit, it wasn't bad. He'd obviously had a lot of practice.

Should she tell Mads about it? Holly didn't want to upset her. But keeping such big news from her seemed wrong.

Sebastiano came out and jumped into the front seat. "Did I miss anything?" he joked, as if nothing could possibly have happened in the last ten minutes in the parking lot of the Carlton Bay Country Club.

"Miss anything?" Holly said. "We're in the parking lot of the Carlton Bay Country Club. What could have happened?"

2 Rules of the Road

To:	mad4u
From:	your daily horoscope

HERE IS TODAY'S HOROSCOPE: VIRGO: I see carnage and mayhem in your future. Oh, wait, that's just the next episode of *Laguna Beach*.

T he rules of the road." Ginny the Gym Teacher—in her new role as Ginny the Driver's Ed Teacher—passed out a booklet of traffic rules and safety tips. "We'll go over them in class, but study them well. You'll be tested on them in your written exam for this course . . . and on the big day down at the DMV."

"I told you this class would be a breeze," Mads whispered to Lina.

Driver's ed met last period Wednesday afternoons. Goth poetess Ramona Fernandez and her acolyte Siobhan Gallagher haunted the back row, while Autumn sat front and center with her friend Ingrid Bauman. Mads hoped she'd never have to share the road with Ramona or Autumn. Autumn struck her as a multi-tasking driver, the type who talks on the phone, applies mascara, fiddles with the stereo, and keeps a lookout for cute guys all at the same time. Ramona was a flirt-with-death sort, and that was one flirtation Mads didn't want to be part of.

"We'll spend some class time learning the rules and the basics," Ginny said. "Then you'll be assigned to practice cars in groups of four with your driving instructor." She indicated the two women and two men leaning against the chalkboard at the front of the room. "This is Jen, Kathy, Doug, and Mitchell."

Mads knew Jen as a gym teaching assistant and Mitchell as a frequent substitute teacher, but Kathy and Doug were new to her.

"Please don't let me get Mitchell's car," Lina whispered. "He subbed for a month last year when Gantner was out having her knee replaced." Mrs. Gantner had been Lina's ninth-grade English teacher. "After lunch he always had food stuck in his mustache."

"Ew."

"Before we start, I want you all to understand what a serious undertaking you're embarking on," Ginny said. "Driving a car is one of the most dangerous things you will ever do—and you'll do it every day. It's like operating a killing machine. If you don't learn to do it properly and keep your wits about you at all times, you could end up like this. Hit the lights, please."

"Oh, no," Lina whispered. "The dreaded crash movie."

"The what?" Mads said.

The video started out okay. A man stood in front of a plain blue wall. "What you are about to see is actual footage from real automobile accidents. You may be shocked, horrified, and upset. You should be. The victims of these accidents were once happy, carefree young people, just like you. They never expected to die in a bloody heap of twisted metal. I imagine you don't, either. But careless driving can have deadly consequences—as you're about to see."

Mads shut her eyes and gripped Lina's hand. "I can't look. You know how I get at horror movies."

The video continued. Mads couldn't see what was happening, but she heard the narrator's voice. "Kenny and Susie were sixteen, out on a date. Look what happened when Kenny took his eyes off the road to give Susie a quick kiss. Just one brief second, and—"

Mads heard tires squealing, a loud crash, metal crunching, gas exploding. She winced. The class groaned. Someone tapped her on the shoulder.

"Open your eyes, Markowitz, or you won't pass this class," Ginny said.

Mads opened her eyes a crack, just in time to see the screen fill with blood and body parts. She shut them again.

Ginny put the video on Pause. "Open them. I'm waiting. . . ."

Mads opened her eyes. The whole class was staring at her. She could understand why. Anything was better than looking at the image frozen on the screen. The top of a car had been sliced off by the bottom of a tractor trailer truck.

"That's better," Ginny said. "And keep them open. I'll be watching you."

The video resumed. Mads' stomach gurgled ominously. She swallowed, trying to keep down the bile. She knew driving could be dangerous. She wasn't the careless type. She'd always be careful—she promised! If only she didn't have to see all this gore.

"Think a stop sign is just a suggestion? Think again," the narrator said as the consequences of running a stop sign were splattered all over the screen.

"Mads, are you okay?" Lina asked. "You look kind of green."

"I think I'm going to be sick," Mads said. "You'd better get out of the way."

She jumped up and ran into the bathroom, making it to a toilet just in time to puke up her lunch.

"Mads?" Lina had followed her in. "Are you all right?"

Mads knelt on the bathroom floor, recovering. "I feel better now."

Lina helped her to her feet, and she washed up. "The movie should be almost over by now. Are you ready to brave the wrath of Ginny?"

Mads rinsed her mouth out one last time, spat, and nodded. "What can she do, toss me under the wheels of a tractor trailer? Let's go."

They slipped back into the classroom. Ginny frowned at them. The movie was wrapping up.

"So the next time you're thinking of speeding, or disobeying traffic rules, or driving while under the influence of alcohol or any illegal substance, remember this: It's a horrible way to die." The narrator looked grim. The words THE END flashed on the screen in red letters.

"Lights," Ginny said. The lights came on. "Do you need to go to the nurse, Madison?"

"No, I'll be all right now," Mads said.

Ginny said. "I'm sorry you got sick, but it shows that the message of the movie really hit home."

It hit home, all right, Mads thought.

"I hope this means you'll be an extra-careful driver," Ginny said.

"Don't worry, I will," Mads said.

Ginny spent the last few minutes dividing the students into practice groups. She chose names at random from the class and refused all special requests. Mads hoped she'd get to be with Lina but braced herself for the worst.

"Car number four: Lina Ozu, Ramona Fernandez, Ingrid Bauman, Karl Levine," Ginny said. "You'll be with Jen."

Mads caught Ramona glancing at Lina, who glanced back. Were they glad to be in the same car, or sorry? It was always hard to tell with them. Mads couldn't figure out whether Lina and Ramona were friends or, if not enemies exactly, antagonists. But they seemed drawn together somehow, in any case.

"Car number five: Autumn Nelson, Martin Irigazzy, Siobhan Gallagher, and Madison Markowitz. You'll be with Mitchell. Okay, that's it," Ginny said. "See you next week."

Class broke up. "I've got the worst car," Mads said to Lina.

"Hey—Mads." Martin Irigazzy stopped her on her

way out of the classroom. She didn't know him well. "We're in the same car."

"Yeah," Mads said. "With Autumn. And Crusty Mustache Man."

"Who?" Martin said.

"It's an inside joke," Lina said.

"Listen, Mads," Martin said. "You barely know me, but—I've liked you for a long time."

Mads was shocked. "You have?"

"Uh-huh. And I was wondering—" He squeezed his eyes shut, took a deep breath, then blurted out, "Do you want to go to the Happening with me?"

The Happening was a dance, the big school event of the spring, coming up in a few weeks.

Mads was too stunned to speak at first. Martin had liked her all this time—and she'd had no idea? How could that happen? She wasn't even sure what his last name was until Ginny read it out loud that day.

She recovered and said, "I'd love to, but I already have a date. I have a boyfriend."

"Oh, that's cool," Martin said. "Just thought I'd ask. Worth a shot, right?"

"Don't worry, Mads," Holly said. "The worst is over. After the first class all you do is drive, pretty much, and that's easy."

Lina, Holly, and Mads headed to Holly's house after school to rehash the day's events. Holly had taken driver's ed the previous fall.

"You wouldn't say that if you knew who's in my practice car," Mads said. "Autumn. And Siobhan. And this guy Martin Irigazzy."

"He asked Mads to the Hap," Lina said.

"Who's Martin Irigazzy?" Holly asked.

"That's what *I* wanted to know," Mads said.

"He's had a crush on Mads forever," Lina said.

"That's wild," Holly said. "All this time he liked you and you barely knew he existed?"

"It's kind of romantic, you know?" Lina said. "Longing for someone from afar. I remember once last year I was riding downtown on the bus with my mother, and I saw this boy walking down Rutgers Street—"

"Uh-oh," Holly said.

"Here we go," Mads said.

"Shut up, you guys," Lina said. "He wore this little Greek fisherman's cap tilted back on his head, and he had all this curly hair and a face that looked like a medieval saint's—"

"Puh. Leese," Mads said.

"Yeah, Mads, it's not as if *you* never idealized a guy," Holly said.

"Thank you, Holly," Lina said.

There was no need to speak the name of The One Mads Held Above All Others, which was Sean Benedetto. Mads knew that Lina and Holly had heard his name enough already.

"Why is it that every story seems to come back to Sean?" Lina said.

"Finish," Mads said.

"I was trapped on a bus with my mother and couldn't talk to him," Lina said. "All I could do was watch helplessly as he walked out of my life forever. I couldn't stop thinking about him. I dreamed about him every night for a week. Even now, whenever I go downtown, part of me is always keeping an eye out for him. But I never saw him again. And I have no way of ever finding him. He's just . . . gone."

"That is so tragic," Mads said.

"There should be a way to find people like that," Holly said. "Like a Missing Persons bulletin board or something."

"Did you ever see those ads at the back of the *Bay Reader*?" Lina said. The *Bay Reader* was a weekly alternative newspaper. "'I Saw You'? People write in things like, 'Girl with braids who works at Zola's—you rock my world.'"

"Oh, yeah," Mads said. "I love to read those. No one is ever looking for me, though."

"Me either," Lina said. "Not yet, anyway. . . ."

"Maybe we could add a feature like that to the blog," Mads said. They had started the Dating Game blog as a school project, but it kept growing. From advice columns to matchmaking quizzes to relationship diaries, it had become the love center of the Rosewood School for Alternative Gifted Education.

"We could call it Missed Connections," Lina said. "You could describe someone you saw in an ad on the site and hope they see it and answer you."

"Right," Holly said. "A girl could post something like, 'Boy who kicked a soccer ball into my face during gym on Friday—I want to get to know you.'"

"'Because I am insane,'" Mads added.

"Or Martin could have written about Mads," Lina said. "'Cute little dark-haired girl with baby face—'"

"Hey!" Mads wasn't fond of her baby face.

Lina ignored the interruption. "'—will you go to the dance with me?'"

"It'll be anonymous, just like 'I Saw You,'" Mads said. "That way, if your crush doesn't respond, nobody will know but you. You don't have to face total public humiliation."

"It's like an online secret admirer note," Holly said.

"Let's do it," Lina said. "For all the Martin Irigazzys out there."

Missed Connections

Do you have a crush on someone from afar, but you don't know his or her name? Did you bump into a cutie in the cafeteria line and want to get to know him or her better? Put an ad in Missed Connections, and get the answers you need! It's anonymous, so if the object of your desire doesn't want to have anything to do with you, no one will know. And you can always tell yourself he or she never saw the ad, so your ego doesn't get completely crushed. Read Missed Connections every day to see if someone is looking for you!

3 Missed Connections

To: linaonme
From: your daily horoscope

HERE IS TODAY'S HOROSCOPE: CANCER: Your altruistic impulses surface today when you try to help someone who doesn't ask for it. Serves them right.

What do you think?" Holly asked Lina. "Should I tell her?"

Lina was stunned. She and Holly walked out of their history class together, whispering. They hardly needed to, the halls were so noisy. Holly had texted Lina a brief summary of Sean's behavior at Autumn's party—basically, the kiss—and asked for advice. Lina was still reeling from the bomb Holly had just dropped.

"I can't believe you didn't tell me this earlier," Lina said. "This happened almost a week ago!"

Holly's mouth twisted, a kind of facial squirming. "I know. I felt so weird about it, and I kept thinking it would go away, but it hasn't. I keep thinking about him. It. What happened."

This will upset Mads, Lina thought. *It has to.*

"If you think about it, nothing really happened," she said to Holly. They stopped by her locker. She put her history book away and got her driver's ed notebook. Driver's ed was next. She'd be seeing Mads in five minutes. She had to compose herself first. Mads could sniff out a secret as easily as brownies. "He kissed you, he asked you out, you said no. End of story. What is there to tell, really? I say don't. You'll only upset her, and for what?"

"Yeah, you're right." Holly looked relieved. "You'd better not say anything."

"Don't worry, I won't," Lina said. "I value my life."

"Why should she be so mad, though?" Holly said. "She has Stephen. Is Sean not allowed to go out with anybody but her?"

"You know Mads," Lina said. "She doesn't have to make sense. She feels the way she feels, and that's the end of that."

"All right," Holly said. "I guess I feel better. What are you doing in driver's ed today?"

"Driving," Lina said. "It's our first day in the student driver cars."

"That's the fun part. Who's in your car?"

"Ingrid, Karl, and Ramona," Lina said.

"Oh," Holly said, making a face. "Oh, well. It's only for a few weeks."

"That's what I keep telling myself," Lina said.

"Have a good class," Holly said. "And remember—what I told you is just between us."

"Got it."

"What a rush!" Mads said as they left the school parking lot. "Don't you love driving?"

Lina glanced at Ramona. Driver's ed was over for the day. Mads had driven like a maniac.

"You almost crashed into our car," Ramona said. "While I was driving."

"Hey, it's my first day," Mads said. "Nobody's perfect the first time out."

"You could have killed us," Ramona said.

"She was only going five miles an hour," Lina said. "I doubt anyone would have been killed."

"I couldn't find the brake," Mads said. "And Mitchell was so busy picking cookie crumbs out of his mustache, he didn't slam on the teacher brake until it was almost too late. That was his fault, not mine! We were all screaming at him, 'Stop! Stop!' His reaction time was shockingly slow."

"All I know is, from now on I'm requesting that our car be as far away from your car as possible," Ramona said. "On the other side of the school if we have to. *At* another school, if necessary."

Lina felt bad. She could see that Mads was hurt. "It was the first day, Ramona."

But Mads had a bouncy, resilient spirit. "Whatever," she said. "Once I get my license, you won't be able to avoid me on the road."

"You're lucky I have a death wish," Ramona said. "Or I'd move to another state after hearing that." Ramona let her dyed blue-black hair fall into her face dramatically. Her long nails were painted green, her lips were purple and pierced, and her dress was black chiffon with a wide silver belt.

"Stop it," Lina said. "Ramona, give Mads a chance. You weren't exactly perfect today. You accidentally put the car into reverse when you were supposed to go forward. *Twice.*"

"Hey," Ramona said. "What happens in the car stays in the car."

"That's a good rule," Mads said.

"Anybody want to go get coffee?" Lina asked.

"I can't," Mads said. "Mom's picking me up out front. Dentist appointment."

"I'll go," Ramona said. "I don't feel like going home yet. Dad's redecorating."

"Okay," Lina said. She and Ramona didn't usually hang out together, but what could Lina say?

She and Ramona unlocked their bikes and rode downtown to Vineland, a favorite RSAGE coffee hang.

"Ugh, look," Ramona said. "The place is full of *them*."

The cozy coffee shop was crowded with different types of people, and Lina found none of them offensive. But Ramona was of a different mind. Almost everyone in the world offended her, just by existing.

They took the one empty table. Lina ordered a cappuccino and Ramona asked for black coffee.

"Did you see the latest *Inchworm*?" Ramona asked. *Inchworm* was a school literary magazine. Ramona was the editor.

"No," Lina said. "Let me guess: You've got a new poem in it?"

"I've got to find material somewhere," Ramona said. "This one's especially good. It's called 'Wheel of Death.'" She then recited:

The Wheel of Death keeps rolling
Rolling, rolling,
Rolling toward us.
Crushing us like bugs under its rolling, rolling wheel.
Man on a treadmill; hamster on a wheel.
Circle of Life, or Wheel of Death?

"That's the first verse." Ramona sat back and smiled, waiting for Lina's response.

"I don't know," Lina said. "You didn't really say anything new."

"Nobody ever says anything new," Ramona said. "There's nothing new to say. It's *how* you say it. The imagery? The irony?"

"You changed the Circle of Life into the Wheel of Death," Lina said. She closed her eyes, pretending to let Ramona's wisdom sink in. She opened her eyes and said, "It just doesn't do anything for me."

"I don't know why I keep expecting you to be different," Ramona said.

Their coffees came. They sipped them to fill the uncomfortable silence. Lina felt that she *was* different from most people, in ways that really mattered. She thought Ramona overestimated her own distinction from the crowd.

"I suppose you're going to that Hormone thing everybody's yammering about?" Ramona said. "With Walker?"

"You mean the Happening?" Lina nodded. "He already asked me, even though it was kind of a given. Are you going?"

Ramona snorted. "No way. Who would I go with? One of these losers?" She glared around the room as if everyone in it were covered with pig vomit. "I'd rather wear pink."

"There must be some guy you'd like," Lina said. "Does he have to be a Goth freak? Maybe you could convert a normal guy."

"Normal is one thing," Ramona said, nodding at a clutch of preppy RSAGE kids. The boys wore crayon-colored alligator shirts neatly tucked into khakis (belted with a shiny leather strap or a blue cotton strip decorated with whales), with polished, sock-free loafers. Two boys even had pennies in their shoes. The girls wore variations of pastel flower-printed tennis skirts, tight headbands or ponytails, simple gold earrings, and more alligator shirts. One girl even wore a pair of red shorts covered in pink turtles.

"But *that* is carrying it too far," Ramona added. "Beyond the realm of White Bread into Stepford land. Is there a planet where they brainwash people so they can't tell a decent outfit from wallpaper? Don't these people know it's the twenty-first century?"

"Some people say the same thing about you," Lina said. "That Goth is so over, so nineteenth century, so fake—"

"I don't care what 'some people' say," Ramona said. "Those people are probably this very group at the table next to us. People who make sure their pants are creased and their part is straight. Why should I take their opinions seriously?"

Lina sipped her coffee. She thought both styles were a little extreme, but she didn't care enough to rant and rave about it. If she liked a person, she liked her, no matter how that person dressed.

"The fashion-y type is almost as bad, though." Ramona was watching a gaggle of popular girls, including Rebecca Hulse, Ingrid Bauman, and Claire Kessler. They leaned together, whispering and giggling. They wore the latest fashions—jeans or short skirts and boots and cute sweaters or jackets—hair long, makeup tasteful. "They're so predictable," Ramona said. "They let a fashion magazine be their bible. If it's in there, you'll see it on them within days. All variations on the same looks, same colors, same shapes."

"I never knew you were so knowledgeable about

clothes," Lina said. "I thought you knew Goth and Goth only."

"You always underestimate me, Ozu," Ramona said. "It's your fatal mistake. See this eye?" She pointed to her heavily eyelinered right eye, which was normally brown but that day was coated by a green contact lens. (The other eye remained brown; Lina could only assume it was on purpose.)

"What about it?" Lina asked.

"It sees all. It knows all. It's the all-seeing eye. Source of my power. Nothing gets past it. If I train it on you—" She opened her eyes super-wide, nostrils flaring, and stared at Lina in a way that was meant to look threatening but really just looked weird. "If I train it on you, it absorbs all your data, and then I have you. You're in my power. The depths of your soul are mine."

"Quit it," Lina said. "You're freaking me out."

"No, you're freaking yourself out."

"What's that supposed to mean?"

"You tell me."

"No, I'm sorry, but you're the one who's freaking me out. Can we change the subject?"

"Fine. I just want to point out that jocks have the absolutely worst haircuts on the planet," Ramona said. "Especially the girls."

"So let's see, you hate preppies, popular kids, and jocks," Lina said. "You like freaks—"

"But only the cool freaks," Ramona said. "Not the wannabes."

"Okay, the cool freaks are allowed to share the planet with you. But out of all those other people, which do you disapprove of the most?"

"Definitely the preppies," Ramona said.

"Why?"

"Because they've elevated Normality to a higher plane. They think it's an art form. They've taken Normality and twisted it until it's almost Weird."

"But wouldn't that make them freaks? Which you would then like?"

"No, moron, because freaks are Anti-Normal."

"But if the Normals are so normal they're weird—"

"Look, you don't get it, so let's just drop it." Ramona stirred her coffee, clanging her spoon loudly against her mug. "It's about *intention*, see, and—"

"I thought we were going to drop it."

"Yeah, okay, you're right," Ramona said. "One day I'm going to write a treatise about this and make you post it on your blog. Just so everyone will understand."

"A treatise. About Normality versus Weirdness. We're not posting that."

"Oh, yes you are. You will if I want you to." She trained her green right eye at Lina, as if it could shoot laser beams.

"Stop it, you look crazy."

"That's the price I pay for my power." Her nostrils flared. "I pay it gladly."

"There are ten more ads today," Lina said. "A lot of kids are out there looking for each other."

She and Holly sat in Mads' room checking on the Dating Game. There were a few new matchmaking requests, a couple of love questions, but the most popular feature was Missed Connections. Lina scanned through the ads while Mads provided them with bowls of freshly popped popcorn. Holly peered over Lina's shoulder.

"'Gorgeous girl with long brown hair, new to RSAGE, wearing tight jeans, boots, a white blouse, and lots of bracelets—I saw you getting a drink from the water fountain in the courtyard Monday afternoon. Your hair kept falling into the water, and you pushed it back with one hand. Did you see me? I was the large guy in the lacrosse jersey who followed you from the courtyard into the lunchroom and then to your econ class, even though I don't take econ. E-mail me! My dream is to go to the Happening with you! Box 3554,'" Lina read aloud.

"Not another Quintana ad," Holly said.

"I keep telling you, that girl knows what's up," Mads said.

Quintana Rhea had arrived at RSAGE a few weeks earlier from L.A. and instantly became the Hot Girl. So far Missed Connections had received thirteen ads that were obviously aimed at her. Lina wondered if Quintana bothered to answer any of them.

Sean was the second most popular Missed Connections target. Three different girls wrote that they'd seen him sing at Autumn's Sweet Sixteen and wanted to go to the dance with him. Sean must have been reading the ads, because Lina came across this entry:

TO MY ADORING PUBLIC

Thanks for all the invites to the Hap, to go to the movies with you, and whatever, but I'm hanging loose right now, not ready to get tied down to one girl, so you can all relax. If I need you, don't worry, you'll hear from me. Lots of luv, S.B.

Lina couldn't resist a glance at Holly to check her reaction. Holly kept cool and didn't betray any feelings. Mads was digging into the popcorn bowl and didn't notice Lina's look.

The door burst open, and Mads' little sister, Audrey, bounced in. "What are you doing, your dumb Web site thing?" she asked, jumping onto Mads' bed and spilling popcorn all over it.

"Get out," Mads said.

"Mom told you not to say that to me anymore, remember?" Audrey said. "You're supposed to say, 'I need my privacy, so please leave the room for now. You may come back later when I'm not busy, and we'll bond like sisters should.'"

"Yeah, and you're supposed to knock before you come in."

"Say it," Audrey insisted.

"Get out," Mads repeated.

"Make me." Audrey lay back on the bed and crossed her ankles, certain of her eventual victory.

Mads stood up, grabbed Audrey by the feet, and tugged. Audrey grabbed the bedspread. As Mads slowly pulled Audrey off the bed, the spread came with her.

"You're making a mess," Mads said.

"*You're* making the mess," Audrey said. "I'm just innocently lying here."

Mads dropped Audrey's feet so they clunked to the floor. "Fine. You want to stay here? Stay. We don't care. Right?"

"Doesn't bother me," Lina said.

"Has anyone been looking for me?" Audrey asked.

"Why would they?" Mads said. "You don't go to our school."

"Some cute boy might have seen me on campus while I was with Mom, picking you up or something."

"And fallen instantly in love with you?" Mads asked. "Is that what you're trying to say?"

"Why not? I'm only eleven, but my style is at least fifteen."

"That's debatable," Mads said.

Audrey hopped up and read the computer screen. "See, that one could be about me. 'Red-haired cutie in cut-offs reading *The Catcher in the Rye* on the front lawn.'"

"You haven't read *Catcher in the Rye*," Mads said. "And you're not a cutie."

"I am, too. And I wear cutoffs sometimes."

"But you don't have red hair," Holly said. Audrey was more of a strawberry blonde. "This ad says the cutie is a redhead. Personally, I think it's Kate Bryson."

"Could be Abby Kurtz," Lina said. "Her hair's red now."

"I don't think he means fire engine red," Holly said.

"He doesn't specify," Lina said.

"Whatever, it's not you, Audrey," Mads said.

Lina read the next ad, then froze.

"Look at this," she said, reading the ad out loud. "'Friday afternoon at Vineland. You: Black-haired beauty in a black dress and boots, silver rings on your fingers, drinking coffee with a friend at the corner table. I really want to meet you but I'm too shy to approach. Me: Boy, eleventh grade. If you're curious, e-mail me at Box 4435.'"

"Is that you?" Audrey asked Lina.

"I'm not sure," Lina said. "I was at Vineland with Ramona on Friday afternoon. We sat at the corner table. And I was wearing a black dress and boots." She held up her right hand, which had silver rings on two fingers. "And rings."

"It's got to be you!" Mads said.

"Maybe," Lina said. "But think about it. What does Ramona wear almost every day?"

"Black dress, black boots, tons of silver rings," Holly said. "And she's got black hair, too."

"By freakish coincidence, I was wearing a black knit shirtdress, and she was wearing a long black chiffon thing," Lina said. "But all Box 4435 says is 'black dress.'"

"Do you think the ad could be for Ramona?" Mads said.

"Wait," Audrey said. "Is Ramona that Goth girl who writes creepy poetry and is always sneering at everybody?"

"That's her," Holly said.

"It can't be her," Audrey said. "This boy likes you, Lina. Case closed."

"Not necessarily," Lina said. "Everyone has different taste."

"Not that different," Audrey said.

"No, really," Lina said. "What if this boy is Goth, too? He could be totally into Ramona."

"Did you see any Goth boys there that day?" Mads asked. "Or any boys checking you out?"

"It was really crowded," Lina said, struggling to remember. "I don't remember anybody in particular. . . ."

"Audrey's probably right," Holly said. "Chances are, this guy likes you, not Ramona. I mean, let's face it, to the vast majority of guys you're the more attractive one. You're pretty, in great shape, you dress nicely, and you don't wear clown makeup to school."

Lina didn't know what to say. She was a modest person, but deep down she knew she was cute, that boys liked her, and that most boys would probably choose her over Ramona. But as soon as she had that thought, she felt uncomfortable and brushed it away. She didn't want to be conceited or assume too much. It wasn't impossible that the ad could be meant for Ramona. She kind of hoped it was.

"It doesn't matter, anyway," she said. "I've got Walker, and I'm not looking for a new boyfriend. So even if this guy likes me, I'm not interested."

"And even if this guy likes Ramona, she probably won't like him back," Mads said. "Doesn't she kind of hate everybody? Even her friends?"

"I don't think so," Lina said. "That's just a pose. I mean, she's a negative person, and she's very critical, but . . ."

Lina wondered if Ramona *would* be interested in this guy, whoever he was. She acted as if the very thought of boys, all boys, was beneath her. But she was a human being. She must crave love of some kind, right? Maybe she was secretly pining for a boyfriend but was too proud to admit it. The more Lina thought about it, the more sure she was that it was true. Ramona protested too much—to hide her vulnerability. In theory.

"We've got to find out who this boy is," she said. "Maybe that will give us a clue about which one of us he likes. And if he likes Ramona, we've got a whopper of a matchmaking case on our hands."

"Ramona and some boy?" Holly said. "That's too much of a challenge for me."

"Me, too," Mads said.

"Not me," Lina said. "I'm going to do it!"

4 Look Out, We're All Going to Die

To: mad4u
From: your daily horoscope

HERE IS TODAY'S HOROSCOPE: VIRGO: You will plumb depths of frustration you never knew existed.

How's driver's ed going?" Mads' father asked at breakfast Sunday morning. "Learning a lot?"

"Yep." She forked eggs into her mouth and focused on her plate. In spite of her bravado, Mads knew her first driving lesson hadn't exactly gone smoothly. She loved the feeling of being behind the wheel and having all those gears and knobs at her disposal, but figuring out what to do with them was so confusing. And the idea of controlling such a big machine was a little scary.

"I heard she practically had an accident the first day," Audrey said.

"I did not," Mads said. "How did you hear that?"

"I didn't," Audrey said. "I just figured you'd suck. Caught you!"

"Audrey, I told you, we don't say 'suck' at the table," Mads' mother, M.C., said.

"Too late, Mom, I just said it," Audrey said. "And so did you."

M.C. looked indignantly at Russell, who shook his head. Mads knew they wouldn't punish Audrey for her smart mouth. *Pathetic*, Mads thought. Her parents were such pushovers. They let Audrey get away with everything.

"Well, listen," Russell said to Mads. "You might not know this about me, but I am the greatest driving teacher in the state of California. I can teach anybody to drive."

"Except me," M.C. said. "We nearly got divorced when he tried to teach me how to drive a stick."

"The thing is, I'm already taking lessons," Mads said. "So I don't really need—"

"How about a little practice session today?" Russell offered. "It can't hurt."

"Well . . ." He was right: An extra lesson might be just what she needed. By her next class she'd be sure of herself, comfortable. Maybe she'd even be the best driver in her car. If only Mitchell's mustache wasn't so distracting . . .

"I've got a couple of hours free this afternoon," Russell said. "We could stop for ice cream afterward."

"And pick up something nice for dinner tonight," M.C. said. "I'm working on my new play today, and it would be a big help if I didn't have to cook."

"All right," Russell said. "We'll stop off for a roast chicken or something. What do you say, Mads?"

"Okay, Dad. Thanks."

"I want to go, too," Audrey said.

"No," Mads said. "You'll get in the way."

"But you're getting ice cream!"

"We'll bring some back to you," Russell said.

"Russell, it would be great if you could take her," M.C. said. "I could really make some progress if you were all out of my hair for a couple of hours."

"Mom, no!" Mads cried. She was looking forward to some rare time alone with her father. Besides that, Audrey always ruined everything.

"Please, honey," M.C. said. "It would mean so much to me. She'll just sit quietly in the backseat and not bother anyone, won't you, Audrey?"

"Quiet as a mouse," Audrey said.

"She's never quiet as a mouse," Mads said.

"I'll be quiet as a mouse," Audrey repeated.

"It's all right, Mads," Russell said. "We'll be fine. And I'll have a nice outing with my girls."

"Great," Mads muttered.

"Okay, turn the ignition," Russell said. The Volvo sat in the school parking lot, Mads in the driver's seat, Russell riding shotgun, and Audrey in the back. Mads turned the ignition key toward her. Nothing happened. "No, turn it *this* way," Russell said, guiding her hand. "That's it."

The car hummed to life. Mads sat up straighter.

"Now, put your foot on the brake—that's right," Russell said. "And put the car into drive."

Mads moved the gear lever. Okay, the car was in drive. So far, so good.

"Good. Now slowly let your foot off the brake and very lightly touch the gas pedal."

Mads lifted her foot off the brake. Her sandal got caught under the gas pedal. She yanked it out, landing on the brake again. The car lurched slightly.

"Look out, we're all going to die!" Audrey yelled.

Russell turned to the backseat. "Audrey, remember, you promised to be quiet."

"I can't help it," Audrey said. "I've got to say something when my life is at stake."

Mads tried to ignore her, but it was hard, so very hard.

"Come on, Mads," Russell said. "Lightly step on the gas."

Mads lightly stepped on the gas. The car rolled slowly forward.

"Good, good."

"You're driving over all the parking lines," Audrey said. "This is totally illegal."

"That's all right, Audrey," Russell said. "This is just practice."

The Volvo purred along. "Go a little faster," Russell said. Mads pressed harder on the gas, and the car zoomed forward. "Not that fast," Russell said. Mads slammed on the brake. The car stopped short. She felt Audrey bounce against the back of her seat.

"Ow! I think I wrenched my neck!" Audrey wailed.

"Are you wearing your seat belt?" Russell asked.

"Yes."

Mads turned around to look. Audrey was sitting there completely unbelted. "You're lying!" Mads cried.

Audrey rubbed her neck. "I didn't think I'd need one for driving around a parking lot at five miles an hour," she said.

"Put it on, Audrey," Russell said. "You should always buckle up whenever you get into a car, no matter how fast it's going."

Audrey buckled her seat belt. "I'm going to make you give me your new velvet jacket," Audrey said. "If you don't, I'll sue you. I've got whiplash."

Mads bristled. She'd just bought the cutest brown velvet shrunken blazer. She knew Audrey had her eye on it. "Go ahead, sue me. You're not getting that jacket. And I'm never letting you borrow it, either."

"Dad, can I sue her? I think I'm going to have to wear one of those neck brace things."

"If you sue her, you sue me," Russell said. He was a lawyer, so he knew about those things. "So no, you can't sue her."

"Did you think he'd say yes?" Mads asked. "'Go ahead and take her for every penny she's got'?"

"I want that jacket."

"Girls, can we get back to work here?" Russell said. "Audrey, quiet back there, or you don't get ice cream."

"What—?"

Russell put a finger to his lips, shushing her and trying to get her to believe he meant business. Mads knew there was no way he would deny his beloved younger child ice cream.

"Okay, Mads. You ready to take a turn?"

"Ready."

Mads practiced right and left turns. She practiced

backing up and saw Audrey crossing herself. When she drove over a curb, Audrey covered her eyes in terror. Mads knocked over a trash can while vertical parking, causing Audrey to scream. The longer the practice session went on, the sloppier Mads' driving became. Audrey was making her crazy. She could feel her father seething with frustration in the seat beside her.

"Concentrate, Mads. You're not focusing."

"Why don't I just crash the car into a tree and put us all out of our misery?" Mads said.

"No! She'll really do it. I don't want to die!" Audrey cried.

"I think we've had enough for today," Russell said, unbuckling his seat belt. "I'll take over from here."

He drove them to Harvey's Carry-out for ice cream cones. When they got home, Mads' mother smiled and said, "I had such a productive afternoon. How'd you all do?"

No one answered. Russell, Mads, and Audrey scattered to their respective rooms and shut the doors behind them.

"Mads, no!" Stephen snapped. "You can't do a three-point turn in six points. It's not the Star of David turn. It's a *three-point* turn."

"I don't see why I can't do whatever I need to to get the job done," Mads said. "As long as the car gets turned around somehow."

Another driver's ed class had come and gone, and Mads had driven Mustache Mitchell to tear a few strands off his face. She wasn't stupid. She wasn't uncoordinated. She was a good dancer, passable in gym, excellent in art, got good grades in almost every other subject. So why did she have so much trouble with driving? It seemed to take her twice as long as everyone else to catch on to it.

So she had asked Stephen for help. Which was looking like a bad idea. Anything was better than another torture session with her father—or so she'd thought. But once locked in a car with a student driver, Stephen was turning into Russell before her eyes.

Three-point turns had given her trouble in the last class, so Stephen borrowed the driver's ed cones and went to the school parking lot to help her with them. A three-point turn was supposed to turn the car around 180 degrees in a narrow space, like a dead-end road. Mads needed at least six moves to get the car around, and she knocked over every cone while she did it.

"The thing is, Mads," Stephen said in a controlled, calm voice she found a little scary, "on your driving test you're going to have to do it *in only three turns*. Once you have your license, you can do it in a hundred turns if you want. If you want to drive everybody crazy. But not when I'm in the car with you."

"I'm sorry," Mads said. "You're making me nervous. I can tell that you're about to blow, and I keep waiting for the explosion. Why don't you just get it over with?"

"You want me to blow?" Stephen asked, his voice still level.

"Not if you're not going to . . . but if you *are* going to, then do it!"

"Aaargh!" Stephen opened the car door, got out, slammed the door shut, and stalked across the parking lot. He talked to himself and stamped his feet. Mads watched him nervously, wondering what he was saying. Maybe he was pretending to yell at her—things he was too chicken to say to her face. And, honestly, she didn't want to hear them to her face. She was sensitive to criticism.

He walked back to the car, taking deep breaths, and got in.

"I'm better now," he said. "I think."

They sat in the car, side by side, the motor running. Mads was afraid to say or do anything. She knew she'd flub the next driving maneuver she tried, whatever it might be, and he'd be ready to explode again.

"You want to try the turn again?" Stephen asked.

"Not really," Mads said.

"Then what do you want to do?"

Silence.

I need to change the subject, Mads thought. *Cut the tension. Put the pressure on* him *for a change.*

Something had been on her mind. Sean. Singing at Autumn's party. She couldn't stop thinking about it, the way he'd held the mike and danced around. . . .

But Sean wasn't her boyfriend. Stephen was.

"Hey, Stephen," she said. "How come you wouldn't sing at Autumn's party?"

Her question obviously caught him off guard. "I-I already told you," he said uncomfortably.

"Are you really that shy? About singing, I mean?"

"Yeah, I guess."

"But how come?"

"I don't know, Mads. I'm just not a good singer. I don't want to make a fool of myself in front of everyone."

"But lots of people can't sing, and that doesn't stop them from doing it in public," Mads said. "Look at karaoke bars. Or even TV."

"I know," Stephen said. "It's just not me."

"But why?"

"I don't know."

"I bet you're a pretty good singer," Mads said.

"I'm really not."

"Better than you think you are."

"I stink."

"Prove it."

"No."

"Come on," Mads said. "Singing is one of the most fun things in life, and you're missing it! It doesn't matter how good you are. It just feels good. Try it."

"Mads, don't."

"We're sitting in a car in the middle of an empty parking lot," Mads said. "You can sing as loudly as you like, and no one will hear you. What have you got to lose? Give me one good reason you shouldn't."

"I don't feel like it."

"Yes, you do. What songs do you know?"

"I don't know any songs."

"Yes, you do. Everybody knows at least one song. Do you know 'My Bonnie Lies over the Ocean'?"

"No."

"Do you know 'Three Times a Lady'?"

"Ick. No."

"Do you know 'Jingle Bells'? You must know 'Jingle Bells.'"

"I don't want to sing 'Jingle Bells' in the middle of spring."

"All right, you tell me. What song do you know?"

Stephen hesitated. There was a song on the tip of his tongue, and he wanted to sing it—Mads could tell. She held back, knowing that to press him too hard just then might mean losing the moment.

"I do kind of know one song," he said. "You know that scarecrow song from *The Wizard of Oz?*"

"'If I Only Had a Brain'?" Mads said. "I love that song. I know it by heart. Audrey watches the movie about once a week. She wants to play Dorothy someday."

"My father used to sing it around the house when I was little," Stephen said. His parents were divorced, and he didn't see his father much anymore. "So whenever I watched the movie, I would pay special attention to that song."

"So sing it!" Mads said.

"No. I'll ruin it."

"I want to hear it." Mads put a hand on his arm and looked into his eyes. Deep down he wanted to sing. He just needed to know that someone wanted to listen.

Stephen cleared his throat. He started off quietly and quavery at first, but his voice grew stronger as he sang. He knew every word. And he had a nice voice—plain, sincere, not always in tune but close enough.

He knocked on his head for emphasis—*knockety-*

knockety-knock—after the line about wanting a brain.

Mads laughed and knocked on her own head, too. "That was great!" She kissed him when he was finished. It wasn't anything like the way Sean sang, but it had its good points.

His face was flushed, but he looked happy. "Do you feel like driving anymore?" he asked her.

"No," she said.

"Let me drive, then," he said. "We're getting out of here."

They switched places, and he drove her home. He whistled the song on the way, knocking on his own head and hers as if they were empty as melons.

5 Sean Tries Again

HERE IS TODAY'S HOROSCOPE: CAPRICORN: If you're wondering why a certain someone likes you, I've got news for you: Everybody else is wondering, too.

"H ey. I got you something."

Holly had been staring spacily at the back of her locker, not even focusing on a picture of Orlando Bloom she'd taped there. Startled out of her reverie, she turned around to find Sean offering her a plastic sprig of holly.

"It's for your car," he said. "To replace the daisy that asshole stole from you."

Holly took the sprig. "Thank you. You're so sweet to remember that."

"Hey. That's the way I roll. I can do thoughtful."

"It's very real looking, for plastic," Holly said.

"I thought about getting you a real piece of holly, but I thought it would just die, and then you'd have to get something else. I didn't want to give you a gift that would just be a pain in the ass."

More evidence of thoughtfulness, of a sort. "Thanks, I love plastic plants. I try to take care of real ones, but they always die. My mother says I have a black thumb." She held out her right thumb as if to show off its major killing power.

"Looks perfectly innocent to me," Sean said. "But I know what you mean. I hate watering plants and stuff. Who needs it, right?"

"Exactly," Holly said.

"So, I know you were busy and couldn't go out with me a couple of weeks ago, but what about this weekend? Want to catch a band or something?"

Holly twirled the sprig between her fingers. He was asking her out again. He was trying to please her. And he wasn't giving up. He was a gorgeous, popular senior, and he liked *her*. He'd actually listened to something she'd said, remembered it, and acted upon it. It was charming.

She was tempted to say yes, but something stopped her. Going out with Sean could make life complicated. There was Mads to think of, even though deep down Holly thought it wasn't fair for Mads to have dibs on a guy who barely knew she existed when she had a boyfriend of her own. Eli wasn't really a problem; they were keeping things casual, and she felt free to do as she pleased.

But going out with Sean was a very public act. People noticed it. It made you an instant gossip target. And Holly still wasn't sure she liked him enough to have her name linked with his for the next however many days or weeks until he moved on to his next conquest.

Unlike most girls at RSAGE, Holly had no illusions about Sean. She knew she wasn't the first girl he'd liked, and she wouldn't be the last. His relationship with his last girlfriend, Jane, had had remarkable staying power—it had lasted three months. Three months. That was just sad. Yet people still talked about what an amazing record that was and how Jane had managed to pull it off.

Beating a record of three months didn't interest Holly. She didn't want to waste her time with someone who didn't take much of anything seriously. And she couldn't afford to get her heart broken again.

"Thanks, but I've got so much homework this weekend. . . ."

"So? Don't you have time for a little R and R? Everybody needs a break once in a while."

She shook her head. "It's really nice of you, but I can't. Thanks."

Sean grinned, and she could see that he thought she was playing games with him, trying to play hard to get.

"I'm serious," she said.

"Yeah. Okay." He didn't buy it for a second. "See you around."

She watched him walk away. She had to admit that watching him walk was fun. He didn't turn back. He was cool. He knew how the game was played.

A bell rang for her next class, which was study hall. Sebastiano appeared beside her and opened his locker.

"I saw that," he said. "Something's going on between you and Sean. I want to hear all about it, starting now."

He got some books, closed his locker, and they walked to study hall together.

"Okay, Sean asked me out," Holly said.

"And you said, 'Why bother with the date? Let's get it on right here, right now.' Correct?"

"*No*," Holly said. "I told him I was busy."

"Good. Very sensible. You've got to watch out for guys like Sean. They're all about the chase."

"I kind of got that feeling," Holly said.

"Of course, you will give in to him eventually," Sebastiano said. "It's a foregone conclusion."

"What? No, I won't. I've already turned him down twice."

"That will just make him hungrier. This is *Sean* we're talking about. No one can resist him. Even half the *boys* in school are ready to jump his bones, given the chance. And I'm talking about straight boys."

"That's ridiculous," Holly said. "I can resist him. I don't even like him that much."

"What is that ugly thing in your hand?"

"This? It's a plastic sprig of holly. For the vase in my car."

"Did he give it to you?" Sebastiano asked.

"Yes. It's kind of sweet of him, don't you think?"

Sebastiano shook his head. "You're a goner."

"Stop saying that," Holly said. "I'm strong. I am woman, hear me roar."

"Uh-huh. Meow."

"Besides, it would be weird going out with him," Holly said. "Mads would have a heart attack."

"She'd get over it. You can't let that stop you."

"I don't know. . . ."

"Can we talk about my problems for a second?" Sebastiano stopped outside the library door.

"We're going to be late," Holly said.

"For study hall? Like anyone cares. If you were my real friend, you would care more about my heartaches than whether or not you're on time for study hall."

"Okay, what is it?"

"Is something wrong with me?" Sebastiano asked. "Something I don't know about? Do I have a KICK ME sign taped to my back? Stray nose hairs I somehow missed?"

"What are you talking about?"

"I'm decent-looking, right?" Sebastiano said. "I want to say super-godlike, but I don't want to sound conceited."

"You're very handsome," Holly said. "I've always thought so."

"So why can't I get a date for the Hap?" Sebastiano said. "I've been turned down twice already!"

"Who did you ask?"

"Jessica Penn and Brooke O'Reilly."

Holly took this in. Jessica Penn and Brooke O'Reilly were two of the prettiest and most popular senior girls in school. Since Sebastiano was a sophomore, he probably wasn't high on their list of potential dates. Also, they both had über-popular boyfriends who had surely asked them to the Hap already.

"Okay," Holly said. "First, they're two years older than you."

"So? Sean's two years older than you."

"I know, but girls usually mature faster than boys, so they like to go out with guys who are their age or a little older." Sebastiano's face fell. "As a rule. Just as a general rule. Going out with a younger guy is not unheard of."

"Okay, so what's my problem?"

"Well, what about Jack and Hunter, for starters?"

"Those losers? What about them?"

"Those losers, as you call them, are Jessica and Brooke's boyfriends. What I'm trying to say, Sebastiano, is that the problem isn't with you, it's with the fact that the girls you asked already have dates."

"Those guys probably take those girls for granted. They might not have even gotten around to asking them to the dance. So I positioned myself to be ready in case an opening came up."

"It's a strategy," Holly said. "All I'm saying is, if you really want a date for the dance, you might have to lower your standards a little. Try asking a girl who doesn't have a boyfriend. Maybe one who isn't the queen of the school and can pick and choose any boy she wants. It might increase your chances of success."

Sebastiano frowned. "That's going to be hard for me. I don't like to compromise." He suddenly brightened. "What about Quintana? She's hot."

Holly shook her head. "Low probability." She knew from all the Missed Connections chatter about Quintana that she had to be taken by now.

"If I'm going to go through all the trouble and hellishness of a school dance, there's got to be some payoff," Sebastiano said. "I won't go with just anybody. I'd rather stay home and watch *Lizzie McGuire* reruns. And you know how I feel about that show."

Holly felt sorry for him. She could see he was experiencing real pain over this.

"I know," she said soothingly. "You'll find a great date. But why not make things easier on yourself? At least ask someone who's available."

"But all the good girls are taken. They always are."

"It seems that way," Holly said. "But even good girls break up with their boyfriends once in a while. And you'll be there to swoop in, catch them on the rebound, and take advantage of their vulnerability. Okay?"

Sebastiano nodded.

"Feel better now?"

"Yeah. Thanks, H."

Holly was surprised Sebastiano cared so much about a school dance. It wasn't like him. He usually held himself above things like that. But maybe he was changing.

QUIZ: IS HE OUT OF YOUR LEAGUE?

You've got a crush on a super-cute guy. But are your hopes realistic?
Do you have a chance with him, or is it the Impossible Dream?

1. He is the star of the boys' soccer team. You are:
   a ▶ the star of the girls' soccer team.
   b ▶ the star of an upcoming feature film.
   c ▶ the star of a puppet show you put on in your basement.

2. You are a straight-A student. He is:
   a ▶ an A student.
   b ▶ a dropout.
   c ▶ a nuclear physicist.

3. A modeling agent stops him on the street and asks him to model. She turns to you and says:
   a ▶ And what about you? You could be an actress.
   b ▶ Nice to see you again, Gisele.
   c ▶ We also handle animal acts.

4. You're head of the cheerleading squad. He's:
   a ▶ captain of the football team.
   b ▶ lead singer of a hot new band.
   c ▶ Chief Gorilla of the King Kong fan club.

5. His last girlfriend was the Homecoming Queen. Your last
    boyfriend was:
    a ▶ school president.
    b ▶ Orlando Bloom.
    c ▶ your teddy bear.

6. When you told your friends about him, they said:
    a ▶ Good for you—you'll make a great couple.
    b ▶ Uh, okay, good luck with that. (While making the crazy sign
        next to their ears.)
    c ▶ He goes to our school? We've never heard of him.

Scoring :

If you picked mostly As, you and your crush are well-suited for each
    other. There's no reason you can't make it work.

If you picked mostly Bs or Cs, then either he's too good for you or
    you're too good for him. The balance of power is off. This
    probably won't work unless the two of you are stranded on a
    desert island together. Stop dreaming about him, and find
    someone who's more your speed.

6 Dear Missed Connections Boy

HERE IS TODAY'S HOROSCOPE: CANCER: Cancers love to nurture their friends. Pity their poor friends.

Not that I read your stupid blog or anything," Ramona said to Lina one afternoon in gym. They were playing dodgeball, and Ramona and Lina had already been eliminated. They sat contentedly on the sidelines watching the hard-core players duke it out. "But did you see that ad from the guy at Vineland?"

Lina stiffened. This subject made her nervous. "I saw it."

"It had to be one of us, right?" Ramona said. "I mean, a black-haired girl, the same day we were there, and he described what I was wearing exactly. Of course, the description could have fit you, too."

"But he was probably talking about you," Lina said. "Don't you think?"

"Yeah, probably," Ramona said.

"It doesn't really matter to me, anyway," Lina said. "I mean, I'm not available. I've got Walker. I'm not interested in anyone new. So whoever this guy is, you know, you can have him."

"Hey, don't try to palm some loser off on me," Ramona said.

"I'm not," Lina said. "I'm just saying that if you like the guy, I won't stand in your way."

"How could you, since the guy obviously likes me?" Ramona said. "Or, you know, he probably does."

"I think so, too," Lina said. It was a *white* lie, and those were okay.

"So what's the problem?"

"Nothing's the problem."

"Okay then."

With a pointed black-purple talon, Ramona picked a scab on one of her chubby knees. Gym clothes didn't suit her. Her sneakers, an uncool brand, were a size too big, like floppy clown shoes, and one of her kneesocks sagged at her ankle. Her cakey white makeup, wild black hair, talonlike nails, heavily lined eyes, and dark burgundy lips all called for something a little more dramatic than baggy black gym shorts and an equally baggy pink top with RSAGE printed across the front. It was the standard gym uniform. Everyone had to wear it. It didn't flatter anybody. But on Ramona it was a form of culture clash. It was like pulling back the curtain and seeing the ordinary man pretending to be the wizard. It was a little more behind-the-scenes information than most people wanted.

Ginny the Gym Teacher blew her whistle. "Round two! Everybody up! Let's go!"

"Why are we playing dodgeball today, anyway?" Ramona asked as she hauled herself to her feet. "Isn't this supposed to be a little kids' game?"

"I guess Ginny couldn't come up with anything better," Lina said. They were supposed to be outside learning various track-and-field events, but it was raining.

"It's better than weight lifting, I suppose," Ramona said.

Ginny herded them into the center of the basketball court. Dash Piasecki and Keith Carter stood poised at either end of the gym, ready to annihilate them with the dodgeball. Ramona didn't bother dodging; it didn't hurt that badly to get hit, she said, so it wasn't worth the trouble. She was the third person out.

"See you on the sidelines," she said to Lina.

Lina worried as she dodged Dash's missiles. Would Ramona answer the Missed Connections ad? She pretended she wasn't interested, but Lina knew she had to be curious, at least enough for one meeting to find out who the guy was.

But what if the guy liked Lina, not Ramona? What if he said so and hurt Ramona's feelings? Lina knew she shouldn't care, but she did. A hurt Ramona was a mean Ramona. A rampaging Ramona. And Lina would be standing right in her path.

Besides, Lina hated to see people get hurt, even people like Ramona, who enjoyed watching others suffer. She was sure Ramona's bravado was hiding something—insecurity, or a secret wish. . . .

I'll check him out first, she thought, ducking a lame throw by Keith. *If I'm the one he likes, I'll let him down gently. Then, somehow, I'll keep Ramona from meeting him.*

That way Ramona would never find out that the boy preferred Lina. Ramona could cling to the illusion that *she* was the girl the boy had liked all along.

Thonk! The ball belted her on the side of the head while she wasn't looking. "You're out, Ozu!" Dash shouted.

"I know, I know," Lina mumbled. She ambled to the sidelines and sat next to Ramona. Ramona's other sock had fallen down, and Lina spotted a blurry skull-and-cross-bones drawn on her ankle in red marker.

What kind of boy would like Ramona? There had to be one out there somewhere. Maybe the Missed Connections boy was the one.

Lina wrote:

Dear Eleventh Grade Boy, I saw your ad. I was at Vineland on the day you mentioned, wearing black, etc., and am curious to meet you. How about after school tomorrow—say 4ish—at Vineland? Let me know. –Black-haired Girl.

She received an answer right away.

Dear Black-haired Girl, I can't wait to meet you. See you at Vineland tomorrow. I'll be sitting at the table next to the fireplace.

The next day Lina, purposely not wearing black, went to Vineland and scanned the room. A boy was sitting near the fireplace, watching the door as if waiting for someone. But no, that couldn't be the Missed Connections boy.

His straight, dark-blond hair was cut in a short, side-parted, traditional style, and he wore a white button-down shirt tucked into khaki trousers. Those shiny loafers, tassels, no socks. And, yes, a whale belt. Gulp.

He wasn't Ramona's type, that was for sure. He wasn't even Lina's type. He was clean-cut and preppy, the kind Ramona hated most.

Lina approached his table. The boy's face lit up in a moment of anticipation, then settled into a brief look of disappointment. He was too polite to let his disappointment show for long, but Lina wanted to see more of it. It was a good sign.

"Hi." Lina sat down beside him. "I'm Lina."

"I'm Rex," the boy said. "Rex Atherton." He shifted his weight. "I have to be honest with you—you're not the girl I expected."

Lina smiled. "I appreciate your honesty. Was the girl you were hoping for a Goth girl? Ramona Fernandez?"

Rex nodded. "Don't get me wrong. I think you're way cute and everything, it's just—"

"It's all right," Lina said. "I was hoping you'd like Ramona. I already have a boyfriend." *And I'm so glad*, she thought. She made a mental note to bring Walker a box of Jujubes next time she saw him, as a token of her appreciation. Walker loved Jujubes.

"So what are you doing here?" Rex asked. "Didn't Ramona want to come?"

"I think she does," Lina said. "I just wanted to make

sure she was the one you meant in your ad. The description could have fit either of us, you know."

Rex laughed. "I didn't think of that. I was so fixated on her, I didn't even notice you—what you were wearing, I mean. I'm sorry . . . I'm so rude. . . ."

"Rex, please, don't worry about it. I'm happy that you like Ramona."

"So—she doesn't have a boyfriend or anything?"

"Ramona?" Lina stopped herself from laughing. "Um, no. She's between boyfriends just now."

"That's a relief," Rex said. Lina took him in again, from the crease in his pants to the neatly combed hair, and was baffled.

"Um, Rex, if you don't mind my asking, what is it exactly that you like about Ramona so much?"

"Oh, I know what you're getting at," he said. "I probably don't look much like the type she usually goes for, right?"

Lina nodded. *To put it mildly.*

"Well, a few weeks ago I was going through a really hard time. I mean really hard. I had these hamsters, see, Hamlet and Ophelia."

"Hamlet the hamster," Lina said, slightly horrified.

"Yeah. They had just had a litter of babies. I hadn't even had a chance to name them yet." His face clouded. Obviously something bad had happened to those baby hamsters.

"That's a shame," Lina said.

Rex nodded. "One morning I woke up to the sound of the hamster wheel squeaking, squeaking, squeaking, over and over. I got out of bed and—well, it was just . . . carnage."

"Carnage?"

"Hamlet had gone on a rampage," Rex said. "He'd killed Ophelia and eaten all the babies. Hamster fur was spattered all over the cage. And Hamlet was running on his wheel, as if trying to sweat away the guilt."

"Sweat away the guilt. A hamster," Lina said.

"After the rampage I couldn't get Hamlet to eat. He wouldn't get off the wheel. He kept running and running . . . finally he escaped from his cage—I don't know how. I never saw him alive again."

"What happened?" Lina asked.

"He was crushed by my little brother's Big Wheel," Rex said.

"Ew," Lina said. "What does all this have to do with Ramona?"

"I'll tell you. I went to school that morning, really upset. I tripped over a pile of magazines. It was the new issue of *Inchworm*. I'd never read it before, but something made me pick up a copy that day. I sat in the courtyard and flipped through it until I came to a poem that made me stop short."

"A poem?" Lina asked. At last she could see where this was heading.

"A poem," Rex said. "'Wheel of Death,' by Ramona Fernandez." He reached into his pocket and took out a neatly folded copy of that very poem. He handed it to Lina.

"That's okay, I've already read it," Lina said.

"Then you see the connection," Rex said. "Wheels . . . death . . ."

"I get it," Lina said.

"I read the poem over and over. It was as if Ramona could see right through my skin. I had to meet her. I asked around, and someone pointed her out to me in the lunchroom. At first I was kind of shocked. I mean, the hair, the makeup . . . she's kind of extreme. But then I realized that only someone so extreme could have written that poem. I realized I have a soul. Because of Ramona."

Lina swallowed. She was speechless. She hadn't expected Rex to be so . . . so . . . *intense*.

"She's not interested in me, is she?" Rex said. "Please Lina, you have to help me. Help me win Ramona's heart."

Lina had never thought she'd hear a boy say those words. And yet, it had happened.

Lina swallowed. "Sure," she said. "Sure, I'll help you."

Maybe Ramona would learn to like Rex. Maybe he

was just what she was looking for, in her secret heart of hearts. How could Lina know?

Or maybe she'll eat him alive, Lina thought.

That seemed more likely.

I wanted a challenge, Lina thought. *Now I've got one.*

7 High-Low

So guess what," Sebastiano said. "I asked Natasha Brearly to the Hap this morning!"

"And . . . ?" Holly braced herself. Natasha Brearly was yet another unattainable girl. At least she was a junior, not a senior, and thus only one year older than Sebastiano.

"Holly!" Sean whizzed down the hall on a skateboard, pasting a sticker on Holly's forehead as he passed. Holly reached up and pulled off the sticker as Sean turned around and skateboarded back to her.

The sticker was a pink heart that said U R HOT.

"I found it inside a valentine some girl gave me last February," Sean said. "I thought it described you perfectly."

"To a tee," Sebastiano said.

"Thank you," Holly said. The clumsiness of the gesture charmed her. Clumsiness equaled sincerity. That was her latest boy theory.

"So—you, me, and Sipress's party on Friday. Want to go?"

"Alex Sipress is having a party this weekend?" Holly hadn't heard about it. Alex was a senior, one of Sean's friends. Getting invited to senior parties was hit-or-miss at this point in Holly's popularity saga.

"You didn't know?" Sebastiano said. "Living in social Siberia?"

"Thanks for telling me about it, Sebastiano," Holly said.

Sean eyed Sebastiano warily. "Dude, how come you're always hanging around here?"

Sebastiano spun the dial on his lock. "Dude, this is where my locker is. What do you want me to do, have it moved?"

"Dude, that won't be necessary," Sean said. "So? Holly? Go to the party with me?"

"Can I think about it?" Holly asked. Her anti-Sean defenses were breaking down. But she wanted to talk to Mads before she committed to anything. She'd decided that was the right thing to do.

"Sure, think about it," Sean said. "Call me and let me know. Later."

He skateboarded away.

"As I was saying," Sebastiano said, "before we were so rudely interrupted . . . Natasha turned me down."

"I'm sorry," Holly said. "But she's another one of those girls, you know, who's really popular and has a boyfriend. When are you going to try an *available* girl?"

"When I find one I like," Sebastiano said.

"What about Bridget Aiken?"

Sebastiano shook his head. "Too mumsy."

"Lulu Ramos?"

"Too tough."

"Maybe a freshman. How about Christie Hubbard?"

"Who, that slut who tried to steal Rob from you?" Holly's old boyfriend Rob had briefly dated Christie before realizing she was too boring for him. That was before he dumped Holly for reasons she never could figure out.

"Ancient history," Holly said. "I'm over that now."

"I don't want Rob's castoffs," Sebastiano said. "Anyway, she's too big-boned."

"If you're going to be that picky, you'll never find a date in time."

"I don't see the point in going with someone I won't have fun with. Why bother?"

"That makes sense, I guess."

They walked into the courtyard to take a break in the sun. Mads was sitting under a tree with Stephen. They were humming some old song and knocking each other on the head.

"Look at them," Sebastiano said. "Don't they look happy? The way mental patients look after a lobotomy."

"They do look happy," Holly said, more to herself than to him. "Excuse me. I've got to talk to Mads."

She walked over to the humming couple. "Hey, guys," she said.

"Hey, Holls," Mads said. "Sit with us. It's such a nice day after all that rain."

"Mads, can I talk to you for a second?" Holly asked. "Over by the picnic tables?"

"Sure." Mads got to her feet and followed Holly to an empty picnic table. "What's up?"

"I need to ask you something," Holly said. "It's a little touchy. . . ."

Mads looked concerned. "What is it? You don't have to be shy with me. You can ask me anything."

Holly glanced across the courtyard at Stephen, who had opened a book and was reading. "You guys seem very tight lately."

"We are. We nearly blew up when he tried to teach me to drive, but I saved us by getting him to sing in front of me."

"That's great," Holly said.

"So what did you want to ask me?"

"Well, I was wondering how you would feel if . . . if . . ." It was hard to say out loud. She'd heard Mads confess her love for Sean so many times. How could she bring this up?

"If what?"

"How would you feel if I went to a party—with Sean?" She blurted out the last two words. Maybe if she said them fast enough they'd pass through Mads without hurting her.

"With Sean?" Mads looked stunned. "You mean, like a date? Did he ask you out?"

Holly nodded.

"He did?" Mads bounced a little with excitement. "Why didn't you tell me?"

"He just asked me five minutes ago," Holly said. It wasn't a lie, exactly. He did just ask her to the party. Why mention all the other times he'd asked her out?

"Oh, my God," Mads said. "I can't believe it. Sean asked you out!"

It was hard to read how Mads felt about it. She flushed and seemed excited, but was she excited for Holly in a good way or just emotional, in a bad way?

"So, what do you think?" Holly asked.

Mads turned and looked at Stephen. She took a breath. "What can I say? Go for it."

"It won't bother you?" Holly asked. "I know how you feel about him."

"How could I say no to you?" Mads said. "You're my friend. And I have Stephen. It's silly. Of course you should go! Just promise you will tell me everything. I want to hear every detail. Okay? Do you promise?"

"Of course," Holly said. "I'd tell you everything anyway. Like I always do."

"Awesome," Mads said. "So when's the party?"

"Friday night. Alex Sipress's."

"And you're going to go?"

"I guess so."

"Call me when you get home. Or the next morning at the latest. Okay?"

"I will. Thanks, Mads."

"What are you thanking me for? I didn't do anything."

Mads went back to Stephen, who stopped reading to

talk to her. Holly felt a flush of warmth. She was happy for Mads, that she had such a nice relationship with her boyfriend. And that she was such a generous friend, to let Holly go out with the boy she'd dreamed about for so long. It really was amazing of her.

"How'd she take it?" Sebastiano asked.

"Well," Holly said. "Better than I expected. Very, very well."

"Sean, dude, you made it." Alex Sipress clasped Sean's hand in some kind of dudeshake and nodded at Holly. "Hey there—I remember you. Hannah, right?"

"Holly."

"Yeah, Holly. Grab a beer, and let's start partying."

Sean took a couple of bottles of beer from the fridge, twisted off the caps, and gave one to Holly. He clinked his bottle against hers. "You finally said yes," he said. "I was getting worried there for a minute."

"Just for a minute?"

"Well . . . you did finally say yes."

"Don't make me regret it," Holly said.

"Hi, Sean." Three pretty senior girls gathered around the two of them, trailed by a couple of burly guys. Sean put his arm around Holly, as if to make it clear to everyone that they should respect her as much as they did him.

"This is Holly," he announced.

"Hi, Holly." The girls smiled at her in a way that they never would have if she'd just passed them by at school.

"Hi," Holly said.

"Guess who's out by the pool," one of the guys said. "Dykstra."

"No way!" Sean's arm fell from Holly's shoulders. He started across the kitchen toward the back door. "When did he get back? Come on, Holly, you've got to meet Dykstra."

Holly shrugged and followed him. The whole group trouped outside to see Dykstra, whoever that was.

"We were buddies—like this," Sean said, wrapping two fingers around each other to show his former closeness to Dykstra. "Until tenth grade. Then his family moved to L.A. He's on TV now."

"You mean *Ben* Dykstra?" Holly asked. "From *Pacific Coast Highway*?"

"Yeah. He plays a surfer dude named Waxman. I don't really watch the show that much." He leaned close to Holly and whispered, "It's kind of stupid."

Holly laughed. *Pacific Coast Highway* was a stupid show. Holly rarely watched it herself. But Ben Dykstra had managed to become a teen heartthrob in spite of the show, and every teenage girl knew who he was, whether she watched TV or not.

"Benedetto!" Ben Dykstra slurred in his trademark surfer drawl. A girl was sitting on his lap—was that Shayna Davis?—but he shifted her off to get up and greet Sean.

"Bennie!" Sean said. They did another dude-shake, different from the one Sean did with Alex. This one involved more finger motions.

"Bennie and Bennie!" Ben said.

"That's what we used to be called," Sean said to Holly. "Bennie and Bennie."

"This is Shayna," Ben said.

Holly thought she'd recognized her. She was also a TV actress, mostly in minor parts, but big enough so you'd know who she was.

"This is Holly," Sean said. He pulled over a lounge chair, placed it next to Ben's, and sat down, patting a spot beside him for Holly. The seniors who had seemed so cool to Holly only minutes earlier hovered around, hoping to be included in the conversation between Bennie and Bennie and their dates, who were now the epicenter of the party.

"So, how's old Rosewood?" Ben asked, snuggling against Shayna.

"Same old," Sean said. "Totally boring. Swim team's good—that's about it. I can't wait to graduate and get the hell out of there."

"I hear you," Ben said. "I quit school last year. I've got a tutor on the set, but he can't make me do much. I'm seventeen—what do you want? I've got better things to do—know what I'm saying?" He gave Shayna another squeeze.

"Right," Sean said.

"So you're not going to finish high school?" Holly asked. The question slipped out before she had a chance to stop it. And she didn't really care. But she was curious to hear the answer.

"I'll take the GED—no big deal," Ben said. "It's not like it's hard or anything."

"I took it this year, and I passed," Shayna said. "And I only went up to tenth grade in school."

"She's smarter than she looks," Ben said.

"How about you?" Ben turned to Holly. "What's your story? Cute as usual, bro," he added to Sean.

"I don't really have a story," Holly said.

"She's a cool girl," Sean said.

"How long have you been together?" Shayna asked.

"This is our first date," Holly said. "We actually don't even know each other all that well."

"But I'll be getting to know her real fast," Sean said.

"That's what you think," Holly said.

"That's what I *know*," Sean said.

"Who-o-a." Ben laughed.

"You want to bet?" Holly said. She was enjoying this banter, and the sense that the whole party was half-listening, ready to gossip about the outcome.

"I'll take you on," Sean said. "How do you want to do this? Game of poker?"

"I'm not that good at poker," Holly said.

"How about high-low?" Ben said. "That's like doofus poker."

"I almost lost my virginity on a high-low bet," Shayna said. "Luckily the guy didn't hold me to it."

"Well, I'm not letting Holly out of this one," Sean said. "Sipress!" he yelled toward the house. "Got any cards?"

"I'll go see." Quintana Rhea, one of Holly's few fellow sophomores at the party, ran into the kitchen, where Alex was playing host.

"Now." Sean rubbed his hands together comically. "What should we bet?"

"How about winner takes it all," Ben said with a leer. "If you know what I mean?"

"Sorry, not on the first date," Sean said primly. It was a joke, but Holly appreciated it. It saved her from having to say it. It was, in its own way, a gentlemanly thing to do.

"How about a kiss?" she offered. "A real kiss. If you

win, I'll kiss you, and if you lose, you'll have to wait until I'm good and ready."

"Okay," Sean said. "A kiss. But it has to be good and long and French and all that. What about second base privileges? Can we toss that in?"

Holly shook her head. "Just the kiss."

"Right here? In front of everybody?"

"No. Later," Holly said. "At the end of the night."

"Aw," Ben said. "I wanted to see it."

"It's got to be right here, right now," Sean said.

"All right." Holly rose to the challenge. "Right here." So she'd have to kiss Sean in front of a bunch of people. If she lost. It was kind of embarrassing but kind of exciting, too.

Quintana returned with a deck of cards and gave them to Sean.

"Okay," he said, shuffling the deck. "Here we go. Are you ready? Are you ready for this, Holly? Cause if you're not, if you're chicken, if you're going to back out, say so now. I don't welch on my bets, and I don't like welchers."

"I'm ready," Holly said. "Bring it on."

Sean held out the deck. "Pick a card, any card."

Holly reached into the middle of the deck and pulled out a card. She wasn't sure if she wanted a high card or a low one. In a way, it didn't matter.

She looked at the card. A five. Not great.

Sean picked a card. "One, two, three, show." They flipped over their cards at once. Sean had an eight.

"I win!" Sean cried. "You'd better brace yourself for one hell of a kiss, girl."

"Best two out of three!" Shayna said.

"Oh, no," Sean said. "I won fair and square."

"Come on, best two out of three," Holly said. "For the fun of it."

"All right," Sean said. "But I'm only going along with this because I know I'm getting that kiss no matter what."

He shuffled again, and Holly picked a ten. Sean had a seven. "We're tied at a game each," he said. "One more round."

Holly chose another card. A queen. Almost unbeatable.

Sean chose and showed his hand. An ace. "Ooh, tough loss. But don't worry, this won't hurt a bit."

He settled himself in front of her. The crowd around them was quiet. Someone giggled nervously. Even Sean seemed struck by shyness suddenly.

He moved her hair out of the way.

She sat up straight. "I'm waiting. . . ."

"I like to take my time," Sean said. He shook out his wrists as if getting ready to perform surgery. A few more people laughed.

Holly glanced around at the faces, gleaming in the watery light from the pool. The shadows made it look like a scene from an arty movie. Everyone was watching her and Sean, waiting to see them kiss. It was weird.

"Okay," Sean said.

"Okay."

"You ready?"

"Ready."

"Pucker up now," Sean said. "But not too tight, because I'm going in for the kill."

That broke the tension, and everybody laughed. Sean leaned forward and kissed Holly gently on the lips. She closed her eyes. He put his arms around her and pressed harder. She forgot about all the people watching. Then someone snickered, and she remembered them again. Sean flicked his tongue into her mouth but didn't linger there. She opened her eyes. He pulled away, then gave her one last quick closed-lip kiss.

A few people clapped facetiously. "Way to go, Benedetto," a guy said.

"I was hoping for a little more skin," another guy said.

"What did *you* think?" Sean asked Holly.

"I liked it," Holly said, very quietly.

"She liked it—hey, Mikey!" Ben yelled.

"Woo-hoo!" More laughter and applause.

Holly suddenly felt as if she were at her own wedding and her groom had just slipped the garter off her leg. What a strange thing to have happen on a first date. But not bad. She was looking forward to the sequel a little later in the evening.

"We'll pick up where we left off later, in the car," Sean said. "Without the peanut gallery. Then you'll see some championship kissing."

"I'm sure I will," Holly said. The laser focus of Sean's attention, and everyone else's, made her feel calm and glowing, like a queen.

8 Vehicular Manslaughter

Sean is friends with Ben Dykstra?" Mads asked.
"And he kissed you in front of everybody?"

"Only because I lost the bet," Holly said.

Mads' head was reeling. It was Saturday morning and
Holly had called to report on her date with Sean, just as
Mads had requested. Mads wasn't sure what to expect, but
it wasn't this. She'd been half-hoping to hear that Sean
had ignored Holly all night and left without even driving

her home. But that was not what happened.

She still couldn't quite believe that Sean had asked Holly out—and that Holly had agreed to go. Every time she thought about that, a sharp pain flashed through her gut, so she pushed the thought away. It wouldn't last, she told herself. It would be over soon, and then she could forget about it.

But this—the party, the bet, the TV stars, the kiss— brought the pain in her gut back. And sharpened it. What was that bitter, metallic taste in her mouth?

It should have been me at the party, Mads thought. But she couldn't say it. Holly was her friend. Mads should be happy for her.

"Then what happened?" Mads forced herself to ask.

"Shayna got pushed into the pool, and everybody went swimming in their clothes. Well, some people were in their underwear. Quintana started that."

"Are you kidding me? You and Sean and Ben Dykstra went swimming in your underwear? Together?" *I should have been there. I want to be there right now.*

"It wasn't as great as it sounds," Holly said. "The water was really cold, and there weren't enough towels to dry off with. . . . "

Don't patronize me. "What kind of underwear does Sean wear?" Mads had to know. If she was going to sit there and politely listen to Holly describe the fulfillment of all Mads' dreams as if it were about as special as Pizza Day in the cafeteria . . . she was going to get some dirt out of it.

"Boxer," Holly said. "Black."

"Wow." Sean in his dripping wet underwear. Mads wanted to scream. Why couldn't *she* be Holly? Holly was acting so cool, like it was no big deal. Which drove Mads crazy. *Keep it together*, she told herself.

"So then what happened?"

"Well, the party broke up after a while, and Sean drove me home."

Mads waited for more, but Holly didn't volunteer it.

"Yeah?" Mads prompted.

"That's about it," Holly said.

"Holly, remember, you promised to tell me every detail," Mads said. "Did he kiss you?"

Holly was quiet for an awfully long time. That metal taste in Mads' mouth grew stronger. She reached for a pack of gum.

"He just kissed me good night, that's all," Holly said. *Liar.*

"God, Holly, it sounds so great," Mads said. She nearly bit her tongue off in frustration. "So do you like him?"

"He's okay," Holly said. "I need more time to get to know him, I guess."

Oof. That pain again. Right through the gut.

More time. To get to know Sean. What a terrible hardship.

"Are you sure you're okay with all this?" Holly asked.

"Yes. Sure. Of course." Mads chomped on her gum. *Holly is my friend,* she told herself. *I can't be petty. I can't be selfish. I have Stephen.*

And she has Sean.

But I have Stephen. And he's a great guy.

But he wasn't Sean.

Why was Holly even asking if it was okay? She knew it wasn't. She should have known, anyway.

If she was my friend—really my friend—she'd know how much this is killing me.

"Are you going out with him again?" Mads asked.

"Yeah, to the movies, next weekend," Holly said. "He wants to see that snowboarding movie. I said I'd go."

"Oh. Sounds like fun." Mads was seething with jealousy. *Don't let her hear it,* Mads told herself. *Keep it out of your voice.*

"I'll give you the full report," Holly said. "But it probably won't be very exciting. Just a movie about a bunch of guys bumming around in the snow."

"Yeah, you'll be bored stiff," Mads said. "And I mean b-o-a-r-d stiff. Ha-ha." *See how cool I am? I can still make a joke while my heart is cracking in half.*

"Good one, Mads," Holly said. "Call me later."

"I will."

Mads hung up the phone. Then she buried her head in her pillow and screamed.

"Okay, Madison, one more time." Mitchell's mustache, adorned with a small dot of mustard, twitched in frustration. It was a slight twitch, but Mads caught it. The feelings of her car-mates were expressed less subtly.

"O-o-h-h-h," Autumn sighed. "Mads, why do you have to be such a total lame-o?"

"Really, it feels like we've been practicing parallel parking forever," Siobhan said. "You're always the last one to catch on."

"She'll get it," Martin said. "She mastered the three-point turn, didn't she?"

"It took her the whole lesson," Autumn said. "The rest of us never even got a chance to try it."

"And when we finally did, at the next lesson, it took us each about two seconds to figure it out," Siobhan said. "Except for Mads."

It was true. Mads was not a natural driver. Especially with people watching her. Any people. It made her nervous. And when she was nervous, she always screwed up.

On top of that, she felt shaky. All the time. If she let

her mind wander for a second, a terrible image popped in. Holly and Sean, kissing. She pushed it away, but it kept coming back. She had to guard against it at all times. It made concentration difficult.

"I can offer you private tutoring," Mitchell said. "Then you won't take up so much of everyone else's time. I only charge fifty dollars an hour."

Mads knew her father would never want to pay fifty dollars an hour for lessons she was supposed to be getting for free. "I can do it this time, I swear," she said. "Set up the cones again."

Mitchell had set up cones to show her where to put the car. He was trying out a new method on her. He told her to aim the car at one cone, then stop; back up to the next cone, stop, and so on. Mads crushed all the cones every time. The last time she'd ended up with the car half-parked on the sidewalk.

"Forget the cones," Mitchell snapped. "That's not working. How about this." He opened the trunk of the car and pulled out two crash test dummies. He stood in front of the car; then, nervously, as if he'd just realized what kind of danger he was in, stepped off to one side. Mads sat behind the wheel, window rolled down. Mitchell shook one of the dummies.

"This is your mother. Okay?" He shook the other

dummy. "And this is your father. If you don't parallel park correctly, you will run over these dummies. Your mother and father. They will die. Do you understand?"

Mads felt like crying. Why was he doing this to her? Threatening to kill her parents only made her more nervous.

He set up the dummies, one in front of the car, one behind. They represented the space Mads had to park between. Then he got back into the teacher's seat.

"Okay. Pull up alongside your mother. Then back up, turning the steering wheel toward the sidewalk, without hitting the sidewalk or running over your father back there. Got it?"

Mads nodded. Her hands were shaking. She didn't want to be responsible for her parents' vehicular manslaughter, even if it was only pretend.

Mads pulled up alongside the mother dummy, then backed up slowly, turning in toward the sidewalk. But she was too far away from the curb, so she pulled forward again and ran over her mother.

"Do we have to sit here and watch this?" Siobhan said. "I've got better things to do."

"Really," Autumn said. "I'm afraid Mads' bad driving is going to rub off on me. We spend so much time watching her screw up, it's making an imprint on my brain. How will I ever pass the driving test this way? Do you *know* what I got for my birthday? A BMW convertible! Do you really think I want to tootle around in it with my dad sitting next to me? No, I do not! I want to go speeding through town with a carful of my friends and honk at cute boys! And if I don't get my driver's license, I'll never be able to do that. Mads, why are you doing this to me? Why are you trying to ruin my life?"

"Quiet back there," Mitchell said. "Or I'll fail all of you. Mads, one more time."

Mads banged her head on the steering wheel. This was her third parallel parking lesson. Her mother had tried to teach her—hopeless. Lina tried to explain it to her, but it only confused her. She'd had trouble with everything else, sure, but she'd eventually figured it all out. All except for this. What was it about parallel parking? Why was it so hard for her?

She tried to park again. By the time she was finished the dummies were completely mangled and the car was about two feet from the curb.

"Again," Mitchell said wearily. "We've got ten more minutes of class time left today. Might as well use it. You won't pass this class if you can't parallel park."

Mads was freaking out. At this rate she'd never get her driver's license.

QUIZ: ARE YOU A GOOD DRIVER OR A FLAKE?
Take this written driving quiz to test your knowledge of the road.
Pay attention now!

1. Which of the following are dangerous to do while driving?
   a ▶ talking on a cell phone
   b ▶ putting on makeup
   c ▶ checking out hotties
   d ▶ all of the above
   e ▶ huh?

2. You are driving on the freeway. The vehicle in front of you is a large truck. You should:
   a ▶ speed up and pass him.
   b ▶ slow down.
   c ▶ keep one car length behind him.
   d ▶ do that hand signal to make him honk his horn.
   e ▶ what?

3. You must notify the DMV within 5 days if you:
   a ▶ lose your driver's license.
   b ▶ move to a new address.
   c ▶ dye your hair purple.
   d ▶ break up with your boyfriend.
   e ▶ I don't understand the question.

4.   It is illegal to park your vehicle:

a ▶ in a loading zone.

b ▶ in front of a fire hydrant.

c ▶ in your neighbor's swimming pool.

d ▶ all of the above.

e ▶ Could you repeat that?

5.   With a Class C driver's license a person may drive:

a ▶ a car.

b ▶ on the grass.

c ▶ underwater.

d ▶ other people crazy.

e ▶ I'm sorry, I wasn't listening.

6.   Unless otherwise posted, the speed limit in a residential area is:

a ▶ 25 mph

b ▶ 55 mph

c ▶ 75 mph

d ▶ whatever speed you happen to be going

e ▶ There's a speed limit?

Scoring: Add up your points, then read the answer that applies to
   you below.

1   a-1, b-1, c-1, d-0, e-5

   2   a-3, b-2, c-0, d-4, e-5

   3   a-5, b-2, c-4, d-4, e-5

   4   a-1, b-1, c-1, d-0, e-5

   5   a-0, b-4, c-4, d-4, e-5

   6   a-0, b-4, c-4, d-4, e-5

0-3 points: You know your driving rules pretty well. The real test should be a breeze.

4-15 points: You're a little shaky on your facts. Better brush up on them.

15-29 points: You have no common sense. You're going to be a menace on the road!

30 points: You're completely out of it. I hope you like your skateboard, because you're going to be riding it around town for a long time.

9 Ramona and Rex

To: linaonme
From: your daily horoscope

HERE IS TODAY'S HOROSCOPE: CANCER: If you really want to help your friends, try secluding yourself in a cave for the rest of the year.

Are you nervous?" Lina asked.

"No," Ramona said. "Should I be?"

Her voice was pitched a few notes higher than usual, Lina noticed. Ramona would never admit it, but she was nervous.

So was Lina. It was Saturday evening and Ramona was about to leave for her meeting with Rex the Eleventh Grade Boy. Lina had called to see how Ramona was feeling about it. She felt responsible. She was the matchmaker. The happiness of Rex and Ramona was in her hands.

Ramona didn't know that Lina had already met Rex. She didn't know that Rex was a super-straight preppy. Lina hoped that Rex would charm Ramona into seeing past their differences and melt Ramona's cold heart.

"What are you going to wear?" Lina asked.

"What do you mean?" Ramona said. "What I always wear, plus a few extra rings."

"How can you possibly fit more rings on your hands?" Lina asked.

"Left thumb. Toes," Ramona said. "Nose, ears, lip. Lots of places."

"Okay," Lina said. "Well, good luck. Have fun. Hope you like him. And be nice to him, okay?"

"I can't make any promises," Ramona said.

Lina hung up. She was planning to go out with Walker later, and she had instructed Ramona to call her on her cell as soon as the date was over. As it turned out, Lina heard from Ramona within half an hour.

"Are you out with Walker yet?" Ramona asked.

"No, I'm still home," Lina said. "I haven't even started dressing yet. Where are you calling from?"

"Home."

"Home? What happened? Didn't he show up?"

"He showed up, all right."

"And?"

"I took one look at him and wanted to turn around and walk out," Ramona said. "I hated him on sight."

"Oh, Ramona."

"But you would have been proud of me. I didn't walk out. I gave him a chance, just like you told me to. I sat down, introduced myself. He's ultra-preppy, Lina. My worst nightmare."

"So? Just because he's preppy, does that mean he's impossible to like?"

"Yes."

"Then what happened?"

"He said, 'Nice to meet you,' and I said, 'Well, it's *not* nice to meet *you*.'"

"Ramona. You call that giving him a chance?"

"He gave me a bunch of flowers—*pink* roses, which I totally hate. I got up, said, 'I'm out of here,' and walked out."

"You just left him there?"

"What choice did I have?"

Lina rubbed her face in frustration. "You had lots of other choices. One of the best might have been to politely say thank you and ask if he wanted to get something to eat."

"That's not something I'd say. I've got to be true to myself, Lina."

"So you're not interested in him at all?"

"Lina, he was wearing khaki pants with a crease in them," Ramona said. "And a pink shirt—what's with this guy and pink? And those horrible whales on his belt! I could barely look at him. He's friends with all those country club people, those Kips and Chips and girls named Sterling. He's a monster!"

"But he likes you!"

"So? What do I care? Does that make me somehow obligated to like him back?"

"No," Lina said. "But you might try getting past the superficial to see what kind of person he is inside."

"I can see what kind of person he is, very clearly. A person who wears whale belts. That's all I need to know."

Lina sighed. Why did Rex's outside have to be so different from his inside? If Ramona would just talk to him for ten minutes, she'd see that they were soul mates.

"Why did you go?" Lina asked. "What were you expecting?"

"I don't know," Ramona said. "An adventure?"

"You'd like to have a boyfriend," Lina said. "Or at least a date to the Hap. Admit it."

"No. I won't admit it."

"But it's true. Right?"

"I've got to go."

A-ha. "See you at school Monday," Lina said.

"Yeah, okay. If I make it in. Five minutes in the presence of a super-prep is enough to make me sick."

Lina hung up. Ramona's stubbornness annoyed her. But Lina had known this would be a challenge when she took it on.

She started dressing. She and Walker were planning to hang out at his house and babysit his little brothers. It wasn't exactly a dress-up occasion, but she didn't want to wear what she had on, which was sweats with a hole in the knee and a baggy T-shirt.

She glanced at her computer. She had a new e-mail.

Lina—Have you talked to Ramona? She met me at the
     Marina, but then she walked off. She hardly talked to
     me! What did I do wrong? Did she say anything? Please
     help me. Rex

If Ramona wanted a boyfriend, she'd have to be more open-minded. It wouldn't be easy to find another boy who liked her as much as Rex did.

Rex—Don't give up yet. Keep at her. Get in her face.
     Sometimes perseverance works. Maybe she'll
     change her mind. Lina

It was a lame strategy, barely a strategy at all. But for the moment Lina couldn't come up with anything better.

"Ramona, this is for you." Lina and Ramona were studying in the library when Rex walked up and gave Ramona a small brown box wrapped in a pink bow. Lina vowed to say something to him about losing all the pink.

"What is it?" Ramona asked, as if she expected the answer to be "dog doo."

"Chocolates," Rex said. "*Dark* chocolates."

Ramona's eyes flashed happily for a split second. *That's the way to do it, Rex,* Lina thought.

Ramona opened the box and took out a chocolate. She bit into it, then spit it out.

"Ugh, there's cherries inside them," she said. "I hate chocolate-covered cherries." She dumped the box onto the table and buried her head in her book. "You can have them, Lina."

"Ramona!" Lina nudged her with her elbow. "You're so rude."

"What?" Ramona said. She looked up. "Oh. Thanks a ton, Rex. You want to make me fail my geometry quiz?"

"I'm sorry, I didn't realize you were studying for a test," Rex said.

"Well, I am, so go away."

Rex walked away. Lina took a chocolate-covered cherry.

"Why are you so mean to him?" she asked. "He's only trying to be nice."

"He's been bothering me all day," Ramona said. "After lunch I found a note on my locker. Some stupid love poem. He didn't even write it himself. He copied it out of a Shakespeare book. From *Romeo and Juliet*, my least favorite play. So trite. Except for the poison scene at the end—that's good. If he'd picked one of the tragedies, especially a slaughterfest like *Hamlet*, I would have been a little more impressed."

"Let me see the note," Lina said.

"I threw it out," Ramona said. "If I want to read Shakespeare, I've got the Complete Works at home."

"He must like you for a reason," Lina said. "Maybe underneath his clothes he's got a dark soul."

"Soul schmoul. His haircut makes me want to vomit," Ramona said. She put down her geometry book and picked up a music magazine that was lying on the table. "See what he did to me? Now I'm all distracted and can't study." She flipped through the magazine, stopping at a photo spread of a band called Deathzilla, her favorite.

"Oh, man, look at him." She pointed to Donald

Death, the lead singer. His black hair was plastered into a sharp, shiny faux-hawk that made his head look pointy. His face was like a doll's, eggshell white with two red circles rouged onto his cheeks. His eyes were heavily lined and a red sneer was painted onto his mouth. Most striking were the two thick black rectangles tattooed over his eyes where his eyebrows should have been. He was wearing an electric blue latex jumpsuit.

Lina couldn't see the appeal. She didn't like his dirge-y, scream-o music, either. But Donald Death was clearly Ramona's type.

"He changed his eyebrows," Ramona said. "They used to be all pointy." She tore the page out of the magazine.

"That's the library's copy," Lina said. "What if somebody else wants to read that magazine?"

"Shove it, Glinda," Ramona snapped. "This is going into my Love Book."

Lina snatched the page away from her. "No, it isn't," she said.

Ramona looked surprised. "Give me that!"

"No. I'm taping it back into the magazine," Lina said.

The bell rang for the next period. Ramona rolled her eyes and gathered up her books. "I'll just come back later and take it again," she said.

"Go ahead," Lina said. It didn't matter, because the

picture wouldn't be there. Lina had more important plans for it.

"Can I look in the mirror now?"

Lina surveyed her handiwork. Rex stood before her dressed in black jeans, boots, a black T-shirt, and a black jacket, with a couple of studded leather bracelets around one wrist. Lina had dragged him downtown to Rutgers Street after school on Friday for a makeover. He actually owned the black clothes; he'd just never worn them all at once before. The boots were new—she'd ordered him to buy them.

Now they stood together in the local Sephora, where makeup samples were free and plentiful. Rex wouldn't go for the cakey white base, but he let her line his eyes and darken his blond eyebrows. Still, something was missing. She checked the picture of Donald Death, which she'd brought along for reference.

"Lina? Can I look?" Rex asked. She hadn't allowed him near a mirror for fear that he would stop her before she was finished.

"Not yet," she said. She dug a jar of her own hair putty out of her bag and got to work on his *Leave It to Beaver* haircut, the one Ramona found so vomitous. She spiked it out as best as she could.

"There," she said. He was no Donald Death—and really, what sane person would want to be? But the old preppy Rex was gone, buried under a ton of hair goo.

"Can I see now?" Rex asked.

"Um, better not." Lina took him by the arm and pulled him out of the makeup store before he passed another mirror. She didn't want him to freak out.

Lina had arranged to meet Ramona at Ruby's, a café down the street. She didn't plan on showing up, however. Goth Rex would show up instead.

"Do you really think this will work?" Rex said. "It seems kind of silly."

Deep down, she had serious doubts. She said a silent prayer of thanks for Walker—laid-back, easygoing, adorable Walker. No makeover required.

"It's a long shot," Lina said. "But Ramona really likes Goth-y punk guys."

Lina peeked through the plate glass window of Ruby's. Ramona sat alone at a table with a cup of tea.

"There she is," Lina said. "Go!"

She opened the door, gave Rex a shove, and ducked away from the window. She counted to three, then peeked.

Rex stood at Ramona's table. Ramona looked up. She seemed confused at first, as if she didn't recognize him. *Good, good,* Lina thought.

Then Ramona started laughing. Not a good kind of laugh. Head thrown back, mouth wide open, chains jiggling. Rex looked pained. Ramona said something and shook her head. She was still laughing when Rex walked out onto the sidewalk.

"She said I can't pull the Goth thing off," he said. "She called me a poseur."

He stared at his reflection in the plate glass. He tried to rub off the eyeliner. "I look like an idiot."

Lina felt terrible. "Rex, did you ever think that maybe Ramona's not the girl for you?"

"She *is*," Rex insisted. "She just doesn't know it yet. You're not giving up already?"

"Well . . ." Lina said. The thought had occurred to her.

"Don't—please," Rex said. "She'd like me if she got to know me—I know she would."

Lina wasn't so sure.

"You said yourself that sometimes perseverance works," Rex said.

"I know, but—"

"Just help me a little longer," Rex said. "She respects you."

This made Lina want to laugh. Ramona respected *her*?

"You're crazy. But all right, Rex. I'll think of something else."

10 Back to the Pinetop

To: hollygolitely

From: your daily horoscope

HERE IS TODAY'S HOROSCOPE: CAPRICORN: Today's events will be a good test of your patience, tolerance, and ability to throw a left hook.

A ll right," Holly said as she settled into her seat at the Carlton Bay Twin. "Bring on the squabbling sisters and their easily solved man problems!"

"Yeah!" Sean rubbed his hands together in anticipation.

Holly looked at him, surprised. "I had no idea you were such a big fan of romantic comedy," she said.

"I am when it features Cameron Diaz in a see-through nightie."

Friday night, Date Number Two with Sean. The classic movie date. Holly punched him in the arm.

"What?" he protested. "I saw it in the Coming Attractions!"

"I thought it was suspicious when you agreed to see this movie so quickly," Holly said. The snowboarding movie was sold out.

She heard a familiar giggle behind her. Was that who she thought it was? She turned around.

"Mads!" Mads and Stephen were sitting right behind Holly and Sean.

"Hey!" Mads waved. "I didn't know that was your seat I was kicking. That's funny."

How did Mads know that Holly and Sean were going to the movies that night? Oh, yeah, Holly had told her. But she'd said they were going to the snowboarding movie, and this was the romantic comedy. Maybe Mads had been trying to avoid them. It was a coincidence, that's all.

Sean turned around. "Hey there, kid," he said to Mads. "Are you old enough to go to a PG-13 movie?"

Mads stuck her tongue out at him. "What do you think?"

He laughed, just teasing her, and turned back around.

The lights went down. Sean put an arm around Holly. She sat stiffly under its weight, thinking about

Mads sitting right behind her, watching. Staring at his arm. What was she thinking? Did it bother her? Drive her crazy? Did she even notice it?

Relax, Holly told herself. She slid down in her seat for more privacy. Sean's hand tickled her neck. What if he wanted to make out during the movie? How could she do that right in front of Mads?

She didn't want to have to think about these problems while out on a date. She just wanted to enjoy her Friday night.

Knowing Mads was back there distracted her through the whole movie. Just when she started to get lost in the story, she heard Mads giggling or whispering to Stephen, or she felt an accidental kick against her seat. Once Mads even leaned forward and whispered to Holly, "Does Cameron Diaz *ever* wear a bra? It looks like she's got two fried eggs on her chest."

Sean overheard and snickered. Holly just nodded. Talking during movies annoyed her.

When the lights came up, Mads said, "That was good. Did you like it, Holly?"

"Mostly, except for the fried eggs," Holly said.

"I liked the fried eggs," Sean said.

"I'm more of a scrambled eggs fan myself," Stephen said.

"Ew," Mads said. "You don't know what we're talking about, do you?"

"I thought you were talking about eggs," Stephen said.

They walked out of the theater into a warm, starry night. "What are you guys doing now?" Mads asked.

Holly glanced at Sean, who shrugged. "Um, we don't really know," Holly said. "Just drive around, maybe."

"Let's walk down to the Marina and get some hot dogs," Stephen said to Mads.

"Okay," Mads said. "You guys hungry?"

"Not really," Holly said. "We'll see you later."

She pulled Sean away to his car. While he unlocked it, Holly looked back at Mads and Stephen. Mads waved, and they turned and walked toward the Marina.

"Want to hit the Pinetop?" Sean asked in the car. "Play a little pool? Winner buys the loser a beer."

"You're on," Holly said. The Pinetop Lounge was perfect. It was a dive bar on the road out of town that was famous for not carding minors—except for Mads. She'd tried to get in several times and was always caught, even with a fake ID. She was small and had a baby face and could never sneak past the bartender.

When they walked in, Sean waved at a guy sitting at the bar and said, "Huh, new bartender."

The pool table was free. Sean bought two bottles of beer while Holly racked up the balls. Her parents had a pool table in their rec room, and Holly had played all her life. She was pretty good. But Sean didn't know that.

"Winner buys the next round," Sean said. "You want to break?"

"Let's bet on something more interesting than beer," Holly said. "How about this: The winner gets to ask the loser any question she wants, and the loser has to answer it. Truthfully."

Sean chalked up his cue and shook his head. "I don't know. Why did you call the winner a 'she'?"

"Or he. She or he. Whatever."

"What kind of question?" Sean squinted at her. This bet seemed to make him a little uncomfortable.

"*Any* kind of question," Holly said.

"Like, 'Who's your favorite ball player?'"

"Could be."

"What about, 'How many boys have you kissed?'"

"I'd like to know the answer to that one," Holly said. "How many boys have you kissed?"

"I'll tell you that now, so you don't waste your question," Sean said. "Zero. And you can repeat that to anybody you want."

Holly laughed. "You break," she said.

Sean hit the cue ball, and two striped balls went into the pockets. "I'm stripes."

It was a close game. Holly kept up with him, shot for shot. Soon there were just four balls on the table: the cue ball, the eight ball, a striped ball for Sean and a solid for Holly.

Holly knocked her last ball in. She took aim at the eight ball. She couldn't wait to ask Sean a question, though she hadn't decided yet what it would be. She had so many: Had he ever been in love? Who with? Did he sleep with every girl he went out with? What made him get tired of a girl he was dating? What kept him interested? Why did he pick her?

She bent over the table, lining up her cue, when someone playfully knocked against her.

"*Whoops!*" It was Mads, kidding around. "We thought you guys might be here."

Holly straightened up. "Hey. How'd you get in?"

Mads grinned. "I know, right? It's the first time ever!" She lowered her voice and pointed to the bartender. "New guy. Hardly even looked at me."

"Give the girl some room, Mads." Stephen pulled Mads away from the table. "Your friend's about to win this game."

"Oh! Sorry," Mads said.

"That's okay," Sean said. "Distract her all you want."

Holly tried to concentrate, but it had just gotten harder. How did Mads find her this time? Did she make Stephen drive around until they spotted Sean's Jeep? What was up with that?

She took her shot and missed.

"Ha-*ha*," Sean said triumphantly. "I smell victory."

Holly could smell it, too—victory for him. So much for all her questions.

Click, clack, and that was it. Sean won. What would he ask her?

"Want to play again?" Mads asked. "Girls against boys this time? Or me and Sean against Holly and Stephen?"

"I'm terrible at pool," Stephen said.

"So am I," Mads said. "So we shouldn't be on the same team."

"I'll be right back," Holly said. "Mads, want to hit the bathroom with me?"

"Sure." Mads followed her to the dingy ladies' room. "Isn't this fun? It's like a double date."

"Yeah," Holly said. "Listen, Mads. I can't help wondering about something."

"What?"

"Are you sure it doesn't bother you that I'm seeing Sean?"

"Of course I'm sure!" Mads said brightly. "Are you kidding? I'm so happy for you! I think it's so great. It's fun to watch you guys together."

Holly felt guilty and annoyed at the same time. Was Mads telling the truth? How could Holly know for sure? If something bothered Mads, it was up to her to say so.

"Okay," Holly said. "I just wanted to make sure."

"I'm so sure," Mads said.

They both put on some lip gloss and walked out of the bathroom. The new bartender was on his way to the men's room. He stopped and gave Mads a good, long look.

"Hey," he said to her. "How old are you?"

Mads swallowed hard and said in her usual unconvincing voice, "Twenty-one."

"Let me see your ID." He studied Holly, who tried to make herself taller. She purposely didn't smile, hoping that made her look older.

Mads pulled her fake ID out of her back pocket. The bartender squinted at it. "This says you're twenty-three."

Mads laughed uncomfortably. "Oh, right. I keep forgetting. The years just fly by!"

"Sure, they do. Sorry, honey, you're out of here."

"No!" Mads wailed.

"If you're still here when I get back from the john, I'll throw you out myself."

Mads hung her head. "Okay." She and Holly returned to the pool table.

"We've got to go," Mads reported to Stephen, and explained why.

"Poor Mads," Stephen said. "It's just as well. They would have killed us at pool. Sean wanted to bet that the losers had to strip. And I'm not wearing my good boxers. Let's go."

"I never get to have any fun," Mads said as he pulled her away.

"Bye, Mads!" Holly said. "I'll call you tomorrow!"

"So," Sean said, putting an arm around Holly. "Back to business. I believe I won that game of pool, and I get to ask you anything I want."

Holly braced herself. "Go ahead. It was my stupid idea. I'm ready to face the consequences."

"Okay," Sean said. "Here goes. Holly, my question is this: Do you—"

He stopped for a swig of beer.

"Do I what?" Holly asked. Why was he torturing her this way? Did she like him? Did she know how to do a half-gainer off the diving board? Did she gain weight when she ate ice cream? What?

"Do you want . . . Wait, I'm really thirsty." Another swig of beer.

Did she want another beer? Something to eat? To kiss him? To sleep with him?

"Do you want to go to—"

"Just say it!" Holly said.

He laughed. "Okay. Do you want to go to the Hap with me?"

The Hap! He was asking her to the spring dance. Holly hadn't anticipated that. The realization took a minute to sink in, and then it spread a warm, happy feeling all over her.

"Remember, you have to answer truthfully," he said.

"Yes," she said. Why not? She hadn't been expecting to go, because she didn't have a date. Now she did. It would be fun to go to the dance with Sean. "And that's the truth."

"All right," Sean said. "That's done. Another game?"

"Definitely," Holly said. "Same bet. And this time you'd better not lose, because I'm going to find out all your secrets."

"No fair," Sean said. "I went easy on you."

"Yeah, well, I'm not that nice," Holly said.

11 Unteachable

Mads yanked a dress off the rack and showed it to Lina. "How about this one? Do you think Sean would like it?"

"Don't you mean Stephen?" Lina asked.

Whoops. "Right, right. Of course I meant Stephen," Mads said. She held the dress in front of her face so Lina couldn't see her blushing.

The dress was short, tight, and covered in silver sequins. Sean probably would like it, if she knew his taste.

Which she didn't. "Actually, I don't think Stephen would like it at all."

She and Lina were at the Durban Galleria, shopping for dresses for the Happening. Carlton Bay had a few cute shops near the Marina but not enough selection for a big event like this. They'd asked Holly to come, too, but she said she was busy. With what exactly, Mads wasn't sure. But she could guess.

Mads had Sean on the brain. She couldn't stop picturing him and Holly together. Snuggling at the movies, his arm around her. Mads had imagined that scenario so many times before—only with herself in Holly's place.

And now the dance. Holly was going to the Hap with Sean! She knew that had always been Mads' dream, but she still said yes. Had she thought about Mads' feelings for *a second?*

Calm down, be mature. That's what Mads kept telling herself. She had Stephen. She started whistling "If I Only Had a Brain." Knock knock. It was their song now. Dopey, but she loved it.

Mads pulled a red velvet dress off the rack. "Try this," she told Lina. "I totally see you in red."

"All right," Lina said. She handed Mads a sheath of satin on a hanger. "And I see *you* in white."

It was beautiful, a white satin 1930s movie star dress.

Mads never would have noticed it on the rack, but now that she looked at it, she knew it was right.

"It really bothers you, doesn't it," Lina said.

"What?" Mads said.

"Sean and Holly."

"No," Mads said. "I'm fine with it."

"No, you're not. You keep picking out dresses Sean would like, as if he were going to be your date instead of Stephen."

"It's just a habit," Mads said. "I've been clothes shopping with Sean in mind for a year and a half. It's hard to stop. But Stephen's my Scarecrow."

"You're sure you're not upset? Won't you feel weird when you see them together at the dance?"

Yes, Mads thought. "I swear I'm not upset," she said, but her hands were shaking. It was a lie. She was very upset. "Holly's even going to give me a driving lesson tomorrow. She's going to help me conquer parallel parking. She said that was her favorite maneuver. She aced driver's ed."

"She *is* good at parking," Lina said. "She's a natural driver."

"Unlike me." Mads waited a beat, hoping for Lina to contradict her, but she didn't.

"I guess if your friendship can survive a driving lesson, it can take anything," Lina said.

"Right," Mads said.

The worst part was, she was afraid to confide in anybody. She didn't want anyone to think that she didn't like Stephen, because she did. And she knew that if she told Lina she was angry with Holly, it would get back to Holly somehow. If Holly knew, it might hurt their friendship. Or make her feel weird around Mads. She didn't know what to do.

Time to change the subject. "What's happening with that boy who's in love with Ramona? Making any progress?"

"No," Lina said. "I've tried everything to help him. The Goth makeover was a stupid idea. Since then he's sent her lots of notes and e-mails. . . . He even pretended he didn't like her, but he couldn't keep that up for more than a couple of hours. She saw right through it. I don't understand why she won't give him a chance. He's a nice guy, and he's crazy about her."

"Maybe she senses that he's mentally ill," Mads said. "Why else would he like Ramona so much?"

"Stop it," Lina said. "Besides, she likes mental illness. The problem is, she thinks he's too normal for her."

"But he obviously isn't, because he likes her," Mads said.

"Exactly," Lina said. "It's totally Catch-22."

"Cut the wheel to the right," Holly instructed.

Mads tugged the steering wheel of Holly's VW.

"To the *right*," Holly repeated.

Was there a note of impatience in her voice?

Mads tugged the wheel the other way. They'd been at it for an hour now, all smiles at the beginning, but the tension was rising between them. Mads wasn't any closer to mastering parallel parking than she'd been when they started. She had lost all ability to tell left from right, front from back, gas from brake, drive from reverse. Her head was a muddle of anxiety, driving instructions and rules and tips slam-dancing in her brain, completely useless.

And being with Holly didn't help. Every time she looked at Holly or heard her voice, she thought of Sean. And felt that pang. It wasn't easy to focus on driving when you were in constant pain.

"Now cut the other way," Holly said. "Left, left! Harder!" She grabbed the wheel to help Mads out. Flustered, Mads let go. Her hands dropped into her lap. If Holly wanted to do it herself, let her.

The car bumped the curb. "Mads, what are you doing?" Holly cried. "You can't just drop the wheel! You're supposed to be steering!"

"You had it," Mads said.

"But you're the driver!" Holly said.

"Then why were you doing the steering?" Mads asked.

"I was trying to help you," Holly said.

Neither said anything for a minute. Mads could hear her own breathing, and Holly's, over the running motor. She couldn't look at Holly. The space between the two of them felt full of electric energy. Mads was afraid that any move into Holly's space would give her a shock.

"Okay," Holly said. "Let's take a deep breath and try one more time."

Holly took a deep breath. Mads did, too.

"Pull up to the starting point again," Holly said.

Mads shifted the gear and stepped on the gas. The car zoomed backward and rolled over the curb.

"Stop!" Holly yelled. "The brake!"

Mads slammed on the brakes. The car stopped in the bushes.

Mads glanced at the gear. It was in reverse.

"Sorry," she said. "I was trying to go forward."

"This lesson is over," Holly said. She didn't raise her voice, but Mads could tell she was struggling to keep her cool. "I guess I'm not much of a driving teacher. Either that or—"

She stopped. Mads looked at her, daring her to say whatever it was she wanted to say.

"Or what?"

"Or you're unteachable," Holly said. She got out of the car and walked around to the driver's side. Lesson over.

12 Shirtless

Mads, I'm sorry." Holly phoned Mads that night to apologize. "I shouldn't have called you unteachable. Of course you're teachable."

Mads' teachability wasn't the real issue, and they both knew it. Holly hated the way that every conversation with Mads was awkward now. Guilt gripped her stomach at the sight of Mads, at the sound of her voice.

It shouldn't be that way, Holly thought. They were

friends, after all. They couldn't let little things like boys and driving come between them.

"It's okay," Mads said. "I've ended up fighting with every single person who's tried to teach me to drive. So don't worry about it. It's just another driving tiff." She sighed. "I'm completely hopeless. I'll never learn how to drive. I'm going to have to get rich so I can hire a chauffeur."

Mads was letting her off the hook. "That's crazy, Mads," she said. "You'll pick it up. It just takes practice. Once you get it, it clicks, and then it's easy. You'll see."

"But why is it taking so long for me to click?" Mads asked. "Everyone else seems to catch on so much more quickly."

Secretly Holly agreed. Mads had one of those minds that just wasn't meant to operate large machinery.

"Everyone struggles with it, Mads, believe me," she said. "You'll get it. But you need to relax. You're too tense in the car. That's what's causing you trouble."

"I know," Mads said. Awkward silence. "What are you doing tonight?"

Holly hesitated. This was a loaded question. "Nothing," she said.

"You're not seeing Sean?"

She was seeing Sean. She had a date with him that night. But she resented having to tell Mads about it. "We might hang out in town for a while, see what's up," she said. "Nothing big."

"Oh. Well, have fun," Mads said.

Did Holly detect a note of anger in Mads' voice? Sadness? Resignation?

"What are you doing?" Holly asked, hoping it was something good. That way she wouldn't have to feel so guilty.

"I have to babysit Audrey. My parents are going out. Big thrills."

Not good. The guilt gripped Holly's stomach tighter. She tried to keep any sign of it out of her voice.

"Fill me in later," Mads said.

"I will," Holly said. "See you."

"Check this." Sean stopped at a basketball court, all lit up for night games, in Fortuna Park. A gang of high school guys were playing a fiercely competitive pickup game and a small crowd had gathered to watch.

Holly and Sean had parked in town and were walking around with no real agenda in mind. At some point they were going to get something to eat—soon, Holly hoped. She was looking forward to a cup of Zola's oyster chowder. But Fortuna Park lured Sean. It was a small recreation area a few blocks from the Marina, with basketball, tennis, and handball courts, picnic tables, and a gazebo.

The boys sweated and fought over the ball, making hotshot plays and shooting from halfway across the court. Sean watched, mesmerized.

One of the players turned around and called, "Dude, get in here." It was Sean's friend Alex. "We need a ball hog." The other guys laughed.

"For sure," Sean said. He took off his sweater and handed it to Holly. "Be right back."

He trotted onto the court and was soon in the thick of the game. Holly couldn't help admiring him as he played. He was a graceful athlete but gritty, snatching the ball from the opposing players and making impossible-looking shots. The spectators shouted and clapped. She could tell that people were rooting for him, even people he didn't know.

Soon he was soaked in sweat. He took off his shirt. There were a few whistles. Holly caught her breath. His chest was slim but well-muscled. A thing of beauty.

"Hold this, Holls?" He tossed his shirt to Holly. It landed in her lap, wet. She gingerly spread it on the bench beside her to dry.

"Could you move that thing? I want to sit down."

Holly looked up to find Mads' sister Audrey standing

behind her. She was licking an ice cream cone and watching the boys.

"Holly! Hey!" Mads, with a cone of her own, was right behind her sister. "Audrey, you're so rude."

"It's okay." Holly hung Sean's shirt on a parking meter. "What are you guys doing here?"

"We were fighting at home, so we biked into town for ice cream," Mads said.

"It's the only thing that can keep us from fighting," Audrey said.

"We were just wandering around, seeing what's up," Mads said.

Holly wondered if this was really a coincidence, or if Mads had dragged Audrey into town to look for her and Sean. After all, she knew they'd be in town that night, and it was a small town. If you were looking for somebody, it usually didn't take long to find them.

Then Holly felt that guilty grip in her stomach again. *What are you thinking? Why are you so suspicious? So Mads keeps turning up when you're on a date with the love of her life. A girl can't go out for ice cream?*

Sean did a fancy dribbling move and a high, leaping layup.

"Yea!" Mads cheered and clapped. "Go, Sean!"

"This is boring," Audrey said. "Can we go now?"

"We just got here," Mads said. "Finish your ice cream."

"I am finished," Audrey said. "I want to watch the *Desperate Housewives* that we TiVoed before Mom and Dad get home."

"It's her favorite show, but they won't let her watch it," Mads said to Holly.

"Too many adult thee-emes," Audrey said, mimicking her mother in a singsong voice.

"Just five more minutes," Mads said.

Audrey turned to face away from the court. "Those boys are all sweaty. I'm sick of looking at them!"

"I know what you mean, Audrey," Holly said. The game was winding down, but Sean was still showboating and soaking up the attention.

"Well, *I* don't," Mads said.

"Mads, if we don't leave right now, I'll tell everyone you're a bed wetter," Audrey said.

"What? I'm *not* a bed wetter!" Mads cried. "And I haven't been since I was three!"

"So? Once I put it out there, it's as good as true."

"Do you believe her?" Mads said to Holly. "This is what I have to live with every day. Total treachery."

"I'm going to do it," Audrey warned. "I'll stand right in the middle of the court, stop the game dead, and say it. One . . . two . . ."

"Oh, all right, let's go," Mads said. "I hate to give in to blackmail," she told Holly. "But the horrible truth is, she'd really do it."

Audrey smiled sweetly. "Buy me another ice cream for the ride home."

"Forget it," Mads said.

"One, two . . ."

Mads dragged Audrey away. The rest of the crowd was dispersing, too. The basketball players had dwindled to three-on-three. But Sean was still playing his heart out.

I thought we were supposed to be on a date, Holly thought. Her stomach growled. She was longing for oyster chowder. *I've spent more time with Mads and Audrey tonight than with Sean. He's totally ignoring me!*

At last the other guys decided to quit. They took the ball with them, so Sean couldn't practice foul shots or anything.

"Hey," he said to Holly. "You hungry?" He was panting, sweaty, and dirty. She'd almost thought he'd forgotten about her.

"I'm starving," she said.

He picked up his shirt, which was still damp. "Hmm . . . Guess I can't really go into a restaurant like this," he said. "You know what they say: No Shirt, No Shoes, whatever."

He was right; even if he put his shirt back on, he wasn't presentable. "What should we do?"

"Let's go back to my house. I'll shower and change, and we can take another stab at it. What do you say?"

There wasn't much choice. "Okay. But I'm really hungry."

"You can fix yourself a snack at my house while I'm cleaning up," he said. "Do you like anchovy pizza?"

"No."

"Well, I'm sure we've got something else in the fridge."

They drove to his house. It was dark. "My mother's at some kind of meeting," he said. "They usually go out afterward and she gets home late."

"Oh." Holly checked the fridge and grabbed a yogurt. Sean flipped on the TV. A basketball game was on.

"I forgot about the play-offs," he said, staring at the screen.

Holly gave him the evil eye until he looked up.

"Right. I'm supposed to be showering."

He left the TV on and went upstairs. Holly sat down and flipped to another channel. She wondered if Audrey had managed to squeeze in an episode of *Housewives* before her parents got home.

Sean came downstairs a few minutes later, in clean

clothes, his hair still wet. "What's the score?" He picked up the clicker and changed back to the game. He sat on the couch next to Holly. Her stomach growled again. That yogurt had only made her hungrier.

"Can we go eat now?" she asked.

"You're really starving, huh? I'm hungry, too," he said. "You know, it's getting late. Why don't we just stay here and eat? You'll get your food quicker that way."

"I guess. . . ." It was more romantic to go to a restaurant than sit in front of the TV and watch a basketball game, but Holly was up for whatever.

"Sure." He got up and went into the kitchen, which she could see from where she was sitting. He opened the freezer. "I'll just nuke some mac 'n' cheese, and we're all set."

"Mac 'n' cheese?" Holly said.

"You don't like it?"

"No, I like it." So much for oyster chowder.

Sean bustled around in the kitchen. "What do you want to drink? We've got Coke, Diet Coke, cranberry spritzer—"

The phone rang. "Here's a glass. Come get whatever you like."

Holly got up and fixed herself a drink while he answered the phone. "Hello? Hey there. Actually, I'm kind of busy right now. Really? You're sweet. Maybe another time. How about tomorrow night? Homework? You still bother with that? We're seniors. . . ."

He was talking to a girl; she could tell. He'd lowered his voice, but she could still hear him.

He hung up and didn't say anything about who it was. It was none of her business. Still . . .

"Dinner will be ready in literally twenty seconds," he said.

She took her cranberry spritzer back into the den. A computer sat on the desk, screen glowing. She glanced into the kitchen. He was busy getting plates and napkins. She walked over to the computer, just to see what was on the screen.

His e-mail account was open. She just read the subject lines and whom the messages were from. *From: bambi, re: hey, hottie! From: leelee, re: next weekend. From: nola, re: tried to call you* . . .

Girls, girls, and more girls. Well, who could blame them?

"Ten, nine, eight," he counted off from the kitchen. The microwave dinged. She hurried back to the couch.

"Love that mac 'n' cheese." He came in carrying a plate of macaroni, a napkin, and a fork and set them on the coffee table. "That's for you. Need anything else?"

"No thanks."

He returned a second later with his own plate and a bowl of nacho chips. "For a side dish." He settled on the couch for some serious basketball watching. Holly started eating.

"No! No!" He leaned forward and shouted at the TV. "Foul!" He sat back and turned to Holly. "Like it?"

"Mmm-hmm." She nodded, her mouth full of piping hot macaroni.

"Awesome."

He got back into the game. The phone rang again. He reached over to the end table and picked it up. "Y-ello? Hey. Yeah, I'm sorry. I meant to call you, but I didn't have time. Um . . . I was sick. Yeah. No, I'm fine now. Nothing serious. Okay. I'll call you later. All right. Bye."

He hung up. "Maybe I ought to turn the ringer off. I hate all these interruptions. How can I watch the game?"

He turned off the phone. "Now we can relax. Go, go, go! Oh, dude! How could you miss that shot?" Back to Holly: "Are you a Spurs fan?"

"Not really."

Holly stared at the TV until her eyes glazed over. She liked sports; it wasn't that—though basketball wasn't her favorite. And she couldn't care less what happened to either of these teams, the Spurs or the Celtics.

But this was only her third date with Sean. The first two had been great. And then he'd asked her to the dance, which was very romantic. But what kind of date was this? Sitting on the couch watching basketball and eating microwave macaroni and cheese? She had the feeling he was already taking her for granted. He sure wasn't trying very hard to see that she had a good time. He didn't even seem to care.

When the game was over, she asked him to drive her home. In the car in front of her house, she had his undivided attention. At last.

13 The King of Parking

Mads! Did you pass?"

Mads found Lina and Ramona waiting for her outside the driver's ed classroom.

They'd all taken their first driving test that day. Mads had passed the written part, no problem. Then came the driving part.

She did everything pretty well. Head-in parking, three-point turn, backing up, signaling . . . Then came her Waterloo: parallel parking. She ran over the curb twice.

She nearly knocked the muffler off the student driver car.

"No, I failed," Mads said. "Parallel parking."

"Join the club," Ramona said.

"What did you fail on?" Mads asked, glad she wasn't the only one.

"Road rage. I got pissed off and ran over all the cones. Something possessed me. I just wanted to see how many I could knock down."

"It's not a carnival game," Lina said.

"It should be," Ramona said. "Driver's ed is so stupid."

"Did you pass?" Mads asked Lina.

"What do you think?" Ramona said. "Miss Perfect. Now she doesn't have to go to class anymore."

"Don't worry, you guys," Lina said. "You get two more chances before you totally fail the class."

"I don't care about the stupid class," Mads said. "I want to get my license! And I never want to look at Mitchell's mustache and know what he had for lunch again."

"You'll pass next time," Lina said. "You both will."

"I don't see how," Mads said. "Parallel parking is impossible! It goes against the laws of physics. Or nature. Or something."

"Calm down," Lina said. "Do you want to go get coffee?"

"I've got to go home," Mads said. "I'll talk to you later."

She stormed back to her locker to get her jacket. As she left the school building, still in a foul mood, she came across Holly and Sean. There were talking for a few minutes before Sean went to swim practice.

Great. This was all she needed.

She stopped, wondering if she should go around another way. But Holly spotted her and waved. Too late.

"Mads, how did your test go?" Holly asked.

"Crappy," Mads snapped. "I failed."

"Parallel parking?" Holly asked.

Mads nodded and kicked a stone in the dirt. She was boiling with frustration. "It's driving me crazy! I just don't get it! I'll never learn to drive. I can't take it!"

"Kid, you can't parallel park?" Sean said. "It's so not hard."

"Not hard for you, maybe," Mads said. "It's like I've got a block against it or something."

"Maybe it *is* me," Sean said. "I'm an awesome driver."

Holly laughed. "You mean you're *fast*."

"Not just fast," Sean said. "Fast and good. Really good. You should see me on the highway."

Mads felt weird standing there listening to them banter. They seemed to have forgotten about her, as if she were invisible.

"Come on," Holly said. "How many accidents have you had since you got your license?"

"Zero," Sean said. "A few speeding tickets, sure . . . Hey, you don't believe me, do you? Are you doubting my driving supremacy?"

"I'm just saying your skills are not out of the ordinary," Holly said.

"You're out of line, and I'll prove it," Sean said. "Parallel parking is my specialty. I bet I can teach the kid here to parallel park in one easy lesson."

"You can?" A thrill rushed up Mads' spine. This conversation suddenly got a lot more interesting. "No one has been able to do that yet."

Holly frowned. "Including me."

"Well, I can," Sean said. "If I do it, will you admit I'm the King of Parking?"

"I guess so," Holly said.

"Great," Sean said. "When do you want your master class, kid?"

"How about tomorrow?" Mads couldn't believe this was happening. Her day had gone from terrible to fantastic. Sean was going to teach her to park!

"Okay, tomorrow afternoon," Sean said. "I'll pick you up. Holly knows where you live, right?"

"Right. Actually, you've been there before. You came

to a party at my house once." So he didn't remember. So what? This time he wouldn't forget.

"I did? Oh. Well, I guess I can find it. See you around four."

He and Holly walked toward the swim center. Mads went to get her bike. She felt like running and squealing with joy. Sean himself was going to teach her to drive! She was going to be all alone with him—in his car! It was too much.

She tried to walk normally, to stay calm. She didn't want Holly to look back and see how thrilled she was. After all, Holly was dating him now. And Mads was cool with it. Totally cool.

14 The Price of Nice

To: linaonme

From: your daily horoscope

HERE IS TODAY'S HOROSCOPE: CANCER: When you've got a pest, you call an exterminator. When that doesn't work, you move. Start packing.

How did she like the tarot card deck?" Lina asked Rex. She'd gone to the lower level of the library to find a book and found Rex instead, leaning against a stack.

Rex had made a set of personalized tarot cards for Ramona, hoping to impress her. He spent hours drawing and painting the cards. He even made the Empress look like her.

"Here's how she liked it." Rex showed Lina the cards. Ramona had sent them back, ripped up, with a note that said, *I'm not the Empress. I'm the High Priestess.*

Lina sifted through the ruined set. "Ouch. Are you okay? You put a lot of work into these."

"I knew getting her to like me wouldn't be easy," he said. "I'm starting to think it's impossible."

"Maybe it is," Lina said. "There are lots of girls around who'd love a custom-made tarot deck. Why waste all your energy on someone who's so mean to you?"

The stricken look on his face made her backpedal. "I mean, someone who's so not worth it?"

"I still think she's worth it," Rex said.

"Okay," Lina said. "But you're a nice guy. You should be with someone who's nice, too. Nice to you, I mean."

A kind of A-ha! look flashed across Rex's face. *He finally gets it,* Lina thought. *Time to give up on Ramona.*

"*You're* nice," Rex said.

"Thank you," Lina said.

"I mean, you've been really nice to me," Rex said. "You've done so much to help me. . . ."

"I really haven't done that much," Lina said.

"So . . . are you saying I should be with a nice girl . . . like you?" Rex said.

No, no. This was not going the way Lina had hoped.

"Sure, a nice girl *like* me," she said. "As in, *similar to* me. But not me."

Rex took a step toward her. Lina took a step back.

"Why not you?" Rex said. "You're very pretty."

"Thank you, Rex," Lina said. "But you know, I'm actually not all that nice. Just ask any of my friends. And I have no soul at all—not compared to Ramona. She's the one with tons and tons of soul."

"That's not true." Rex took another step toward her. She took another step back. This guy wanted a girlfriend in the worst way. "You've got soul. You wouldn't have helped me if you didn't."

"No, really, I don't," Lina said. "You know what I like? Great big shopping malls. And parking lots full of shiny cars. And fast food! I love fast food and canned, predictable music and remakes of remakes of cheesy movies and McMansions, and anything plastic and—"

He laughed. "See? Your sense of humor proves you've got soul." He took another step forward. She was backed up against a stack with nowhere to go.

"Forget it, Rex. I have a boyfriend. His name is Walker. I like him very much." *Very, very, very, very much.* More than ever, now that she saw the alternative up close.

"Lina, will you go to the Hap with me?"

"Did you hear what I just said? I have a boyfriend. I'm going to the Hap with him."

Rex drooped. "Oh, why do I always like girls who don't like me back? Is it some kind of curse?"

"No," Lina said, "it's—"

She froze. It was human nature. To want something you can't have. Some people wanted the unattainable more strongly than others. Still, it was a human trait. And Ramona was human. Sort of.

"You still like Ramona, don't you, Rex?" she asked. "Deep down? Tell me the truth."

"Sure, I do," Rex said. He began to quote "Wheel of Death" from memory.

"That's enough," Lina said. How could Ramona not love a guy who memorized her awful poems? It seemed impossible. "Don't give up on her yet. I have a new idea."

"But we've tried everything. She doesn't like me."

"She might like you if she thinks she can't have you," Lina said. "If you *pretend* to like me, maybe she'll get jealous."

"That's game-playing," Rex said. "She's above that."

Lina laughed. "I wouldn't be so sure."

"Hey, Lina, I was thinking about the Hap," Walker said. He found Lina later that day, sitting with her laptop in the courtyard, checking her e-mail. "Am I supposed to get you a corsage or something? My mother said I should, but to me it's totally . . . Hey, what are you reading?"

There was no point in hiding it. It was a message from Rex.

> Lina—My heart bleeds for you. It's like a bloody piece of steak. Not the kind you buy at the supermarket, wrapped in plastic. The really super-bloody kind that you buy at a butcher shop.

"Isn't Rex the guy you were fixing up with Ramona?" Walker asked.

"Yes."

"What is he, some kind of weirdo?" Walker said.

"Yes," Lina said.

"So, what, he's into you now? Or he's just hungry for a steak? I don't really get it."

"It's my new matchmaking plan," Lina said. "He's pretending to like me in order to get Ramona jealous. At least, I hope he's pretending."

"But how will she know he's e-mailing these freaky messages to you?" Walker asked.

"I'll show you." Lina pressed FORWARD, then put Ramona's e-mail address in the SEND box.

"Whoops," she said. "My finger slipped."

Then she sent Ramona another e-mail, which said:

Sorry! I forwarded that last message to you by mistake. Just
ignore it.

"Seems like a lot of trouble to go to for a couple of freaks," Walker said.

"I know," Lina said. "But if I don't keep Rex busy chasing Ramona, he'll come after me. I can't handle that."

15 Slurpees

HERE IS TODAY'S HOROSCOPE: VIRGO: Five-star day! To be followed by a negative-five-star day. What goes up must come down.

O kay, the first rule of driving is: You've got to look good in your car. Right? I mean, what's the point if you don't look cool?"

Sean, sitting in the passenger seat of his mother's Honda ("The Jeep's too hard to handle for a beginner," he told Mads), studied Mads' cool quotient. She was sitting up straight in the driver's seat, hands at ten o'clock and two, trying to see over the wheel. And desperately trying to steady her shaking hands.

Sean was sitting right next to her. In a car. So close, she could feel his breath on her neck.

"See, this is all wrong," Sean said. "You can't look so perky in your car. You've got to *cruise.*" He pressed a lever, making the seat rise. "Now you're sitting higher, so you can slouch. Lean back in your seat. Right hand on the steering wheel, left arm resting on the open door window. There you go."

He touched her hand! *Stay cool, stay cool.* "Hey, you're right. I do feel cooler."

"What did I tell you?" Sean said.

The moment had finally arrived: Mads' driving lesson with Sean. The twenty-four hours between his offer to teach her and picking her up at her house had felt like twenty-four years. And she'd spent the whole time deciding what to wear. She tried on every outfit in her closet. She spent three hours on her makeup alone. She was torn between looking fabulous and looking effortless. She ended up somewhere in between.

Now she was alone with him in the car, his attention completely focused on her. The school parking lot had never looked so beautiful. The asphalt seemed to sparkle with stars. From this day forward Mads would always have a soft spot for silver Honda four-door sedans.

"Now, what's the deal here? Parallel parking?" Sean said. "Unfortunately you need to use two hands for that. But you can still look cool."

"Show me," she said.

"I'm about to do that. Let's do a little warm-up drive first. Once around the parking lot. Show me what you've got."

Mads carefully accelerated and chugged around the lot in a long, slow circle.

"Let your arm hang slack. Relax." Sean leaned against her to adjust her arm. He rested his hand on her leg for a second. After he lifted it, the spot felt hot.

"Give it a little gas, girl," he said. "There's no traffic. You've got the road to yourself. Let's see some driving."

Mads stepped on the gas and the car sped forward. "That's right. Feel the wind in your hair," Sean said. "This is what driving is all about."

Mads went faster. She was headed straight for the wall of the school. What would she do when she got there? She didn't know. She couldn't think.

"Okay, slow down, slow down." Sean pressed on her leg to indicate that she should brake. "Head-on collisions with brick walls are not cool. That might pop the air bags, which would really piss off the old lady."

He draped his arm over her seat. He was doing it so

he could see her feet and make sure she was pressing on the right pedal. But Mads didn't care. She sat still for a minute, just to absorb the feeling of Sean's arm around the back of her seat.

"Take us over to the curb, and we'll do the parallel thing," he said.

She drove to the curb where she'd practiced and failed so many times before and got into the pre-parking position.

"Good," he said. "You know how to start, anyway. This is going to be a cinch."

"You don't know what I've been through," Mads said. "I'm such a screwup! I'm always running over the curb or backing up too fast or knocking out the muffler. . . ."

"Hold on," Sean said. "Now listen. You're getting all worked up. We just started. Today is a new day. You haven't screwed anything up yet. What did I tell you? Cool. Be cool. Even if you have no idea what you're doing, don't show it. Pretend you know. Make it look good. It'll all work out."

"But—"

He pressed two fingers to her mouth to quiet her. "You're like a race car driver, see? The greatest girl driver who ever lived. And you're parking in front of the Roadhouse because they're throwing a big party just for you. 'Cause you won the Indy 500 or something. So you take it to the curb, no problem. You don't even think about it. Got it?"

Mads had no idea what he was talking about, but she nodded yes. His fingers were still on her lips. Without thinking she flicked out her tongue and licked them. She didn't know what made her do it—an instinct took over.

"Hey!" He pulled his hand away and laughed. "That's the right attitude. Now let's park this baby."

Unlike all her other tutors, he didn't tell her which way to pull the steering wheel and when to put on the brakes. He just slouched back, one arm out the window, and waited for her to do it.

She backed up, pulled into the curb, and stopped. Then she moved forward, aligning the front end with the sidewalk. She backed up a little to straighten the wheels. And that was it. She did it. She parallel parked.

For a second she was too stunned to say anything. It had been so simple. She sat in the idling car, staring at the wheel.

Sean leaned out the window to see how close she was to the curb. "Awesome. You did it," he said. "I don't see what all the fuss was about."

"I did it!" Mads shouted. "I did it!"

"Yeah, I said that."

She threw her arms around him and gave him a hug. It wasn't a full-body hug because her seat belt held her back. Sean laughed and patted her on the back. "Way to park, kid. I knew you could do it."

"I did it!" Mads shouted again. "You don't understand—that was the very first time!"

"Told you I was a good driver."

"You're the best," she said.

"Do it a couple more times, just to make sure," Sean said.

She pulled into position and did it again. And again and again. She got it. She couldn't understand why it had been so hard for her before. It was just a matter of getting the hang of it.

"Got any other driving problems you need to solve?" Sean asked.

She wished she could think of one. She wanted to stay there with him all day. But on the other hand, knowing she could pass her test now was a good feeling.

"All right then," he said. "Let's go get Slurpees to celebrate. You want to drive to the 7-Eleven?"

"I don't have my learner's permit yet."

"Oh yeah. I guess that would be illegal. Well, I don't need any more trouble in traffic court, so let's switch seats."

She moved to the passenger seat. "Thanks again, Sean. You really saved my butt."

He patted her leg and said, "Glad I could help. There's nothing like saving a cute girl's butt."

He kept his hand on her leg all the way out of the parking lot and down Rosewood Avenue. Mads was afraid to move. She didn't want to do anything to make him take his hand away.

He pulled into the 7-Eleven. Mads felt as if her heart would jump out of her chest. As jittery as if they planned to rob the place. Sean got out of the car and loped to the front door. She scrambled out to follow him.

Inside the store it was cold and smelled like stale candy. Sean poured himself a root beer Slurpee, and she got cherry. She liked the way cherry ices stained her lips red. When it was time to pay, she pulled some bills out of her jeans pocket, but he pushed them away and said, "I got this."

A gift from Sean. She wished she could save that Slurpee forever. She'd definitely keep the cup.

Back in the car, he clinked his plastic cup against hers. "Here's to another wack chick on the road," he said. "Just kidding. You'll be great. How's that Slurpee?"

"Good. Want a taste?"

"Yeah." He leaned over and sipped from her straw. He

made a face. "Cherry doesn't taste good after root beer. Here." He held out his cup for her to taste. She took a sip.

"You're right. Root beer's better," she said. Then she checked her reflection in the side door mirror to see if the cherry was doing its work. Yep, there it was, a red ring around her lips. Better than the best lipstick and worth it even if it wasn't her favorite flavor.

"Let's blow out of here." Sean started the car and headed for Mads' house. He turned up the radio. Rock music blasted through the car, so it was hard to talk. But every once in a while he looked over at her and gave her that heart-stopping smile. It was even more killer close up than at the usual distance.

"I saw you playing basketball the other night," she shouted over the music. "At Fortuna Park."

"Oh, yeah? I was on fire that night."

"You were great! Um, did you ever play on a team?" She was struggling to come up with things to say, to keep his attention on her. She wished this drive could last forever.

"Not since junior high," Sean said. "Swimming's year-round, pretty much. And I'm not tall enough to be *really* good."

"I think you're tall."

"That's 'cause you're a shrimp," he said, but not in a

bad way. He rested his elbow on her head to demonstrate her shrimpiness.

Before she knew it they were on her street, chugging up the hill toward her house. Sean stopped the car but left the engine running. He turned the radio down.

"So, are we cool?" he said. "You got your parking down?"

"Thank you so much, Sean," Mads said. "You really helped me."

"Hey, it was fun." He unbuckled his seat belt. Then he unbuckled hers. "You're a cute girl, you know that?"

"I am?" she whispered.

He was slowly, steadily, moving closer. "Yeah, you are. Come on, you know it. Those pinchable little cheeks." He lightly pinched one of her cheeks. Her pinchable cheeks had always been one of her least favorite features, since, until that moment, they had been admired only by aunts and grandmas.

He touched the dimpled spot right under her nose. "You've got a little red Slurpee over your lip. Let me fix that for you. . . ."

And that's when he kissed her. He kissed her fully and deeply on the mouth. This was no friendly peck. He wrapped his arms around her and pulled her close. She sighed. His breathing got heavy. Her left leg slipped into the gap between the two seats. She half-sat on the emergency brake. She didn't care.

He pulled away slightly, holding her head between his two hands. He touched her hair as if it were silk. She stared at him, wide-eyed and stunned. She couldn't think.

"Good driving today," he said. He ran a hand down her spine and back up again, as if to give her a shiver for the fun of it, because he could. "See you later."

"See you." She sat still, unmoving. *Oh*, she thought, her brain sluggish. *I'm supposed to get out now.*

In a trance she opened the car door and stumbled out. She turned and looked at him. He rebuckled his seat belt and gunned the engine. Somehow she knew that meant she should close the door.

"Bye." She closed the door. He waved, honked, and drove away.

She stood on the sidewalk for a good ten seconds, in shock. *He loves me!* she thought. *Sean loves me!*

That kiss said everything. *He's finally mine!*

All along her street, the trees and shrubs bloomed with flowers. The air smelled like perfume. Why hadn't she noticed it before? Her street was the most beautiful street in the whole world!

She blinked. Sean was long gone. *Go inside,* her dopey brain told her. She walked up the jagged stone steps to her house. Each step looked like a pearl. A pearl button on a wedding dress.

"How was your lesson?" her mother asked. "Did you make any progress?"

Mads nodded. She couldn't speak. She didn't want to break the spell. She went straight to the stairs. She had to get to her room.

"Mads? Are you okay?" her mother said.

She knew she had to answer, convincingly, or her mother would not leave her alone. So she summoned all her strength and squeaked out, "Yes. I'm fine. Just tired."

"Okay," M.C. said, and went back to her book.

Mads closed her bedroom door and lay down. The first shock and joy of being kissed by Sean began to fade, and a flood of new emotions washed over her.

What a great kisser. He was such a great kisser! As she knew he would be. Her mind drifted back to the awkward fumblings she'd shared with Stephen, and she felt sad. There was no comparison. Sean was so much better. But then she felt guilty. Stephen tried. He was so sweet. Maybe he didn't know what he was doing—not like Sean, who was an expert—but he and Mads were learning together. Every time she thought about Stephen she felt a stab of guilt, so she pushed him out of her mind.

She closed her eyes and licked her lips, trying to

relive the kiss. The greatest moment of her life. He said she was cute! And then he kissed her. Like he really meant it. Like he really liked her.

It's fate, she thought. *I've been resisting it for so long. But now it's time to face it.*

I'm in love with Sean.

She'd always loved him. He'd always be the love of her life. She'd thought it wasn't realistic, but that day was proof that she—everybody—was wrong. It was real. He'd kissed her. He liked her! Her dream was coming true at last! All she'd needed was that one chance to be alone with him. He seized that chance and showed her his true feelings.

She felt another rush of joy . . . and another stab of guilt. Not just over Stephen this time. Holly.

Holly was going to the Hap with Sean. They were dating. She was basically his girlfriend. Mads had just kissed her best friend's boyfriend. How could she be so low?

But then, how could she have let Holly go out with him in the first place? How could she have surrendered the love of her life—her true love—to another girl, without a fight? How could she have been so foolish?

The joy was weakening, replaced by anxiety. What was she going to do? She had to clear her life to make way for this new development, for Sean. Should she break up with Stephen? When? What about the Hap?

And Holly. Would Sean tell her he'd kissed Mads? Should Mads tell her? Would Holly ever forgive her?

Evening fell, the room grew dark, but Mads stayed on her bed. She didn't turn on the lights. Suppertime came, and her mother knocked on the door, but Mads pretended to be asleep. She stayed that way all night, in the dark, images and visions whirling through her mind, her mood shifting from excitement to fear and back again. She finally fell asleep on top of her bed, still dressed.

16 Stuffed Hamster

To:	linaonme
From:	your daily horoscope

HERE IS TODAY'S HOROSCOPE: CANCER: You're the calm center of a world gone mad. Just like the bubble gum is the center of a Blow Pop.

You're kidding me." Lina gasped when she heard the news. Mads had called her first thing in the morning. Sean and Mads! "You're lying. You're making this up. Right?"

"It's true," Mads said. "Lina, it was so amazing! He must have kissed me for, like, two whole minutes. I didn't count, but it felt long. And way too short! He's such a good kisser. I feel like I'm on drugs. I can't stop thinking about it!"

Lina didn't want to believe it. But she knew it had to be true. Sean had kissed Mads. And Mads was sure there was more to come. She could be right. Who knew what Sean would do next?

"But, Mads," Lina said, "what about Holly?"

Mads was silent for a minute. Then she said, "I know. I don't know. What should I do? Do you think I should tell her what happened?"

"It would be bad if she heard it from someone else," Lina said. "Like Sean."

"Do you think she'll be mad?" Mads said.

"Well . . ."

"It's not like I set out to kiss him or anything. I didn't plan it. And he started it, not me! How can Holly blame me?"

"When it comes to kissing, people aren't always rational," Lina said. "She could blame you for kissing him back. If you're her friend, you have to tell her. It's the right thing to do."

"Oh, god," Mads said. "She'll never forgive me. She'll hate me forever."

"Mads, this is big," Lina said. "Telling her what happened will probably hurt her, but it might help her, too, in the long run. If she can't trust Sean, she should know that."

"I hate this," Mads said. "Why does everything good

always have to come with something bad? Why can't the good things just happen in a purely good way that makes everybody happy?"

"They just don't," Lina said. "Not this time. What about Stephen?"

Mads sighed over the phone. "I guess I'll have to break up with him. It will be so sad. We're like buddies now. Love buddies."

"You're really good together," Lina said. "Sean doesn't last long with anybody, you know. You could be kicked to the curb faster than you think."

"No," Mads said. "I don't think so. This is fate. The real thing. You know how I've felt about him, ever since I first saw him. What could be more real than that? It took time for him to come around, but that's okay. He's the one for me."

God, she's so delusional, Lina thought. But it was no good telling Mads that—she would never listen. "I hope you know what you're doing," Lina said. "Just be careful."

"I will," Mads said, but Lina knew she wouldn't. Being careful wasn't Mads' way.

"Where did you get that thing?" Ramona reached inside Lina's locker and pulled out a small stuffed hamster that hung by the tail from a coat hook. "Sure is ugly."

"Rex gave it to me," Lina said. She'd suggested he give

her flowers, but he thought Ramona would find the hamster more believable.

"Rex did?" Ramona tried to look uninterested, but Lina could tell she was faking it.

"Yeah. You know, his hamsters died? He said that in a way that's what brought us together."

"In a pretty roundabout way," Ramona said.

"That's what I think," Lina said. "Have you heard anything from him lately?"

"No," Ramona said. "Thank god. I sure am glad I got rid of him. You can have him."

"Great! Thanks!" Lina said.

"Thanks?" Ramona said. "You *want* him?"

"He's growing on me," Lina said. "Sure, he's superstraight and all that, but when he likes a girl, he really likes her. All the way. On the outside he might look dull, but on the inside he's a tiger. Dramatic. All the big emotions swirling around. Being with him is like being in an opera. Or a big tragedy. It's big, big, big."

"I thought you didn't like him," Ramona said. "You like Walker."

"Sure, Walker's great, for a *regular* guy," Lina said. "But Rex is different. He's not like any other guy I've ever known. He's special."

"Rex wants a poet," Ramona said. "A *real* poet."

"Are you implying I'm not a real poet?" Lina said.

Ramona shrugged. "Lately all you write is sports news. Not many people consider that poetry."

"Maybe Rex does."

"So, are you two going to get together?" Ramona asked. "Are you going to dump Walker?"

Lina thought, *A-ha, she does care.*

"Maybe," Lina said. "If things keep going well. And if you really don't want him. But I think he's pretty much over you by now."

"I don't want him," Ramona said. "But he's not over me. Not yet."

"How do you know?" Lina asked.

"No one gets over me," Ramona said. "Not that fast."

Lina smiled. The plan was working. At least, she hoped it was. Ramona acted as if she didn't care. But there was a heart beating somewhere under all that ragged black chiffon.

17 Confession Time

To: hollygolitely
From: your daily horoscope

HERE IS TODAY'S HOROSCOPE: CAPRICORN: Get ready for a good whomp upside the head. Yeah, another one.

Come on, Mads, stop stalling," Holly said.

Mads had come home with Holly after school, saying she needed to talk. But once at Holly's house Mads kept dillydallying, raiding the fridge, putting on music, channel surfing on the TV, asking to see what Holly was wearing to the Hap. Everything but seriously talking. Holly's nerves buzzed; she could sense that something was up, and she wanted to get it over with. "What did you come over to tell me?"

"Is this new?" Mads picked up a large Mayan bowl that sat near the fireplace. "I don't think I've seen it before."

Holly took the bowl out of Mads' hands and put it down. She led her to the couch and forced her to sit. Then she moved the remote out of Mads' reach.

"Stop it," Holly said. "Talk."

Mads squirmed. "Can I have something to drink?"

"No," Holly said. She sat across from Mads, waiting.

"Okay," Mads said. "Remember, I'm telling you this because I'm your friend. You mean a lot to me—so much that I don't want to keep any secrets from you. Especially important secrets. That's how much I care."

"Spill it."

Mads took a deep breath, squeezed her eyes shut, and blurted, "Sean kissed me."

"What?" Holly's pulse quickened. She was suddenly aware of the veins in her wrists.

"I'm really sorry!" Mads said. "I didn't mean for it to happen. I didn't do anything to provoke it, I swear. It just . . . happened."

"When he took you driving?" Holly asked.

Mads nodded.

Of course, it had to be the driving lesson. Sean and Mads alone in the car . . . The idea had made her uncomfortable, but she wouldn't let herself dwell on it. She trusted them, she told herself, both Sean and Mads. Her sort-of boyfriend and one of her two best friends. She should be able to leave them alone together. But it looked as if she was wrong.

There was one last hope, one last way out. "You mean on the cheek, right?" Holly asked, knowing that wasn't what Mads meant.

Mads bit her lip. "No. Not on the cheek."

"A real kiss? A kiss kiss?" She paused. "A French kiss?"

Mads nodded sheepishly.

Holly sat in her chair, squeezing the armrests with her hands, feeling the blood race through her body. An image of Sean and Mads locked in an embrace formed in her mind. It hovered just long enough to make her stomach hurt before she forced it away.

She didn't like *everything* about Sean. But she liked him. She wanted him to like her. And her alone.

She stared at Mads, who looked extremely nervous. Mads could seem sweet and childlike. But that was deceptive. Holly had always known that. She loved Mads anyway. She loved her contradictions. Until now, when they slapped her in the face.

Mads squirmed. She was obviously miserable. This only irritated Holly more. If Mads felt so sorry about kissing Sean, why had she let it happen? Holly knew Mads never tried to stop him. Kissing Sean was Mads' dream. She'd run over her own mother with a Jet Ski for a chance to kiss Sean. It was the great romantic moment of her life. What was Holly's friendship and trust compared to that? Nothing. Dispensable. Expendable. Useless.

Holly rose to her feet. She was so mad, she felt as if her skin were steaming.

"How could you do this to me?" she demanded. "How *could* you? I was open with you. You knew I was seeing Sean. I told you everything. I let him take you out to teach you to parallel park. Don't you think I knew I was taking my chances when I did that? I knew. But did I say a word? No. I thought I could trust you. I knew you'd be alone with the boy of your dreams and you'd probably try something fishy, but I thought, *No, Mads is my friend. She'd never do anything to hurt me. I can trust her.* I'm so stupid!"

"Holly, please!" Mads cried. "I'm so sorry! But what about Sean? Shouldn't you be mad at him instead of me? I mean, he started it!"

"And you put up a big fight, didn't you," Holly said.

"Well . . ."

"You didn't," Holly said. "I know you."

"Holly, I wasn't trying to hurt you," Mads said.

"You weren't thinking about me at all," Holly said.

"You know, I didn't tell you this, but Sean first asked me out a long time ago. Weeks ago. And I said no. You know why? Because I thought it would upset you. Even though you have a boyfriend and you have no claim to Sean at all, no right to keep me or him or anyone from dating anyone, I said no to him because I care about you."

"What made you finally say yes?" Mads asked.

Holly paused. This question didn't fit into the self-righteous speech she was in the middle of making. But it was there, dangling in front of her, and it had to be answered.

"I finally said yes because he kept after me and I started to like him, and I saw how happy you were with Stephen. But before I said yes or did anything, I *asked you*, if you recall. I *asked you* how you would feel about it. And you said you were fine with it. And then, and only then, did I agree to go out with Sean. So you see, I never once forgot about your feelings. I thought about you and how you'd feel the whole time. Meanwhile, any thought of me went out the window as soon as Sean showed up at your door."

"No, Holly, that's not true," Mads said.

She had tears in her eyes, and Holly felt bad for her. She couldn't help it. Holly tried to stay hard, stay angry. She was hurt. Mads had betrayed her. Sean had betrayed her. Did Lina know about this? Or Stephen?

"What about Stephen?" Holly asked. "Have you trampled over him as carelessly as you've trampled over me?"

"I haven't told him anything yet. . . ." Mads said.

"Well, brace yourself, because he'll be hurt," Holly said.

Mads sobbed. Holly couldn't comfort her. Holly felt very alone.

"Mads, I would never do something like this to you," she said quietly.

"I know," Mads said, the tears flowing. "You're such a good friend, and I'm so sorry. . . ."

Holly couldn't stand to watch her cry any longer. Shouldn't *she* be the one who was crying? "Could you just leave now?" Holly said. "I feel like being alone."

"Are you sure?" Mads said. "Maybe I can do something for you. Get you something? Make cookies? Or fudge? I don't want to leave this way, Holly, with you all mad at me. Isn't there some way I can make it up to you? Some way we can be friends?"

"I don't know," Holly said. "Just go now."

She walked to the door and opened it for Mads, who didn't move. Holly stood her ground. Mads picked up her bag and walked slowly to the door, crying. Holly felt sad and angry at the same time. Her heart kept hardening and softening with every beat. She just wanted Mads out of there so she could go to her room and cry in peace.

"Call me?" Mads sniffled weakly.

"Good-bye," Holly said.

She closed the door. She heard Mads sob on the other side. Then she went to her room, closed the door, and turned the music up loud.

18 Zombie Days

For the next few days, Mads walked through the halls of RSAGE like a zombie. Her feelings were muddled, good and bad, but all strong, fighting for dominance inside her. Paying attention in class was impossible. She flunked a geometry quiz. She was constantly on the lookout for Sean, who suddenly seemed scarce. If she caught a glimpse of him, her mood soared. He was the whole reason behind everything that had happened, the reason her life was a mess. It had to be worth it . . . right?

Holly wasn't speaking to her and avoided her whenever possible. Lina seemed torn between her two friends, unsure what to do, trying to comfort them both but not really able to help either one. And Stephen . . . Mads was avoiding him. It wasn't so hard, since she didn't see much of him at school anyway. Normally she missed him, but now she was afraid. She didn't know how to face him. What would he say? Had he heard somehow? Would he take one look at her face and know?

After the fiasco with Holly, Mads wasn't eager to go to Stephen and confess. What would that accomplish, anyway? It would only start a fight. Mads didn't need another enemy. Still, she couldn't lie to him. So whenever she saw him coming, she ducked away.

But on Wednesday he caught her at last. She was leaving the biology lab. He waited for her at the door. She couldn't escape.

He took her by one arm and steered her into a corner. "Hey," he said. "Haven't seen you in a while."

"I know," she said. "Where've you been?"

He half-smiled. "Is everything okay?"

"Sure," she said, too chicken to be honest. "Of course. What do you mean?" On *mean* her voice rose to a suspiciously nervous squeak.

"You've been kind of distant lately," Stephen said. "Never home when I call, never around at school . . . Almost as if you're avoiding me."

"I've been busy, that's all," she said. "So many tests and things . . ."

"Well, I was just wondering if anything was up," Stephen said. His calmness, his patience, were heart-breaking.

"Nothing's up. Really." If she were going to tell him anything, she wouldn't do it there, in the school hallway, in the middle of the day. She didn't want a public scene, and he wouldn't appreciate it either.

"Listen," he said. "I don't know what's going on. But I've got a funny feeling. So I just wanted to tell you that if you don't want to go to the dance with me anymore, that's okay. I'll understand. Just tell me so I'll know."

The dance . . . a complicated issue. Ever since the big kiss, Mads had been waiting for Sean to come back for more. And she was hoping he'd ask her to the dance. But as of now he was going to the dance with Holly. Would he break up with Holly in order to take Mads? Maybe, maybe not. If not, Mads still wanted to go with Stephen. She still wanted a date. But what if Sean asked her? Then she'd have to break it off with Stephen . . . Her head was spinning. Too many *ifs*.

I should tell him, she thought. *So he can ask someone else to the Hap if he wants.*

But standing in front of him, looking at his face, she just couldn't do it. *I'm the biggest chickenhearted loser who ever lived,* she thought, her spirit fading.

"Everything is okay," she told him. "I still want to go to the dance with you. Of course I do."

"Good," he said. But she could see in his face that he didn't quite believe her.

19 Bitter Clarity

| To: linaonme |
| From: your daily horoscope |

HERE IS TODAY'S HOROSCOPE: CANCER: Your life is full of poetry. Really bad poetry.

Bitter Clarity

I offered you my blood,
My heart, my lungs, my liver,
Everything inside me,
My guts a churning river.

We could have freed our minds
We could go joyfully crazy
Feel our way through the fog
Making it even more hazy.

But you refused.
How can you turn away a soul?
You must be ice inside, or stone,
Or all dried up and used.

You could have had all this:
My world of pain,
My sodden brain,
My days of weeping in the rain.
Instead you chose to keep me sane
And leave a stain.

"It's beautiful," Lina said. "So intense."

"I know," Ramona said.

"Who wrote it?" Lina asked. Though she knew the answer very well.

"Rex," Ramona said.

With a little help from me, Lina thought. She almost wished she could confess to Ramona, just to show her that she could write self-indulgent poetry as well as anybody.

Lina sat in the office of the *Inchworm*, watching Ramona put together the next issue. Ramona sifted through a pile of recently submitted stories and poems. Lina had found "Bitter Clarity" on top of the stack.

She'd convinced Rex to submit a poem and helped

him write it. She thought Ramona was jealous enough now to respond.

"It's about me, isn't it?" Lina said.

"Are you crazy?" Ramona said. "It's obviously about me. Did *you* refuse him? No. Did he offer *you* his lungs, liver, et cetra? I don't think so."

"I thought he liked me. But I guess he never got over you."

"I told you, no one ever does," Ramona said.

"Are you going to publish it?" Lina asked.

"I'm deciding," Ramona said.

"If you publish it, does that mean you love it?" Lina said.

"It means I think it has some kind of merit," Ramona said. "That's all."

"Come on," Lina said. "You're not telling the truth. This poem is your taste exactly. Admit you love it."

"No."

"Admit it," Lina said. "Or I'll—I'll burn it. No, I'll flush it down the toilet."

"I'm sure Rex could just print out another copy," Ramona said.

"But you'd have to go ask him for it," Lina said. "Which would be admitting you like it. And you don't want to do that."

Ramona said nothing.

"That would shift the whole balance of power between you," Lina said. "And you don't want to do that, do you? Because you like to make him suffer."

"He's not suffering, is he?" Ramona said. "He likes you now—according to you."

"Only because you won't have anything to do with him. Come on, Ramona. Don't you miss having him to kick around?"

She reread the poem out loud. Ramona's eyes shone.

"Okay, I admit it," Ramona said. "This poem made me see him differently. And I do miss torturing him."

"Then do something about it," Lina said. "Ask him to the Hap."

"Forget it. I don't want to go to the stupid Hap. And anyway, I have my pride."

"You do, too, want to go," Lina said. "And what about your pride? How can a real poet, someone who spills her guts onto a page and prints it out for the whole world to see, how can she be put off by false pride? You should be above that. False pride keeps you from your real feelings. And isn't that what being a poet is all about? Getting past the superficial to the real feelings below?"

"What are you, my therapist? You don't know anything about being a poet."

"I know this," Lina said. "If you were a real artist, you'd take risks. You wouldn't be afraid. You can't always set yourself above everyone else, making sarcastic remarks from on high. Someday you're going to have to let yourself be vulnerable. You have to take a chance on getting hurt, or you'll never really know life, or pain, or death, or all that stuff you're always writing about. Take a chance, Ramona. Ask Rex to the dance."

"Ugh," Ramona grumbled. "You should be on *Oprah*."

"See? That's what I'm talking about," Lina said. "Instead of addressing the issue, you spit out a quick putdown and hope I'll shut up."

"Yes, I do hope you'll shut up," Ramona said. "I'll ask Rex to the dance. Just stop lecturing me."

Lina grinned. *Victory is mine!* she thought. No more annoying Rex. She knew better than to gloat in front of Ramona, though. Ramona could take it all back in an instant.

20 The Tater Tot Treaty

To: hollygolitely
From: your daily horoscope

HERE IS TODAY'S HOROSCOPE: CAPRICORN: You have a friend who cares. Or, as you put it, meddles.

There's Mads," Lina said.

Holly had already spotted her. She and Lina sat on a bench in the courtyard, eating lunch. Mads had stepped from the cafeteria into the courtyard, lunch in hand, looking for a place to sit. As soon as she saw Mads, Holly looked down at her roast beef sandwich.

"Mads!" Lina waved to her, encouraging her to come sit with them.

Why was she doing that? She knew perfectly well

that Holly wanted nothing to do with Mads.

Mads knew it, too. Holly glanced up and saw Mads sussing out the situation. Mads stared longingly at them. She looked sad. She waved at Lina. Then she turned around and went back inside the cafeteria.

"Hol-ly," Lina said, drawing her name out. Holly knew what was coming. If Holly, Lina, and Mads had been sisters, Holly would have been the bossy oldest, Mads the spoiled youngest, and Lina the peace-loving middle child.

"What?" Holly said grumpily.

"Are you really still angry at Mads?" Lina said.

"Yes," Holly said.

"Be honest," Lina said. "Were you actually surprised that something happened between them? You knew how Mads felt about him. And Sean's not exactly a monk when it comes to girls."

Holly grimaced. Lina was right. When it came to girls, Holly didn't put anything past Sean. And when she'd asked for Mads' blessing to go out with Sean, part of her knew that Mads was just *saying* it was okay. Mads didn't mean it; she couldn't. She was trying to be generous, trying to do the right thing for Holly. But she couldn't help her feelings. And Holly had known what Mads' feelings were only too well.

So, yes, Mads had betrayed her. But in a way Holly had betrayed Mads first.

What a mess.

"Let me put it this way," Lina said. "Do you really, really like Sean? I mean, *really* like him? So much that you'll never speak to Mads again?"

This was the real heart of the matter. Holly was losing interest in Sean. She could feel his interest in her draining away, too. They weren't soul mates; she'd never thought they would be. He was sexy, sure, and an interesting challenge for a while. They had a certain chemistry together. But Holly was no match for his relentless self-interest. In Sean's eyes, nobody could compete with himself.

Lina didn't need to hear every thought in Holly's mind. All she needed to know was this: "You're right. I don't like him that much anymore."

"Then why stay angry with Mads?" Lina said. "Make up with her, Holly. She's so upset."

"It's a matter of principle," Holly said. But her resistance was weakening. The fight with Mads was pointless. Holly could see that now. And she missed Mads.

"I understand what happened," Holly said. "Sean is an eye-of-the-hurricane person. He comes through every encounter unscathed but leaves a trail of destruction in his wake."

"Mads is probably sitting alone in the cafeteria, picking at her Tater Tots," Lina said. "You two could be friends again by the end of lunch period."

"I do kind of miss the little squirt," Holly said. She got up and took her sandwich into the lunchroom.

She found Mads sitting alone, just as Lina had predicted. Holly sat down across from her.

"Hi," Holly said.

"Hi," Mads said. She pushed her plate toward Holly. "Tater Tot?"

"No thanks," Holly said. "Listen, Mads—I still don't like it that you kissed Sean while I was going out with him. You know that was wrong, don't you?"

"Yes," Mads said. "I really do. Really really really."

"Okay. As long as that's clear," Holly said. "I'm going to break up with him."

"You are?"

Holly nodded. "He can be fun, but he's not the guy for me. He's too . . . all over the place. So even though you were totally wrong to let him kiss you"—she gave Mads a fierce look to let her know that nothing like that had better happen ever again—"I care about you more than him. So I forgive you. I want to be friends again."

Mads beamed. "I'm so glad! I'm so glad! I'm so glad!"

"You said that."

"It was so horrible when you wouldn't speak to me," Mads said. "I felt like somebody was choking me. I couldn't relax. I couldn't sleep. I felt so guilty. And I missed you so much!"

"I missed you, too," Holly said. "I hate fighting. And I think we were tearing poor Lina in half."

"Yeah, she hates being caught in the middle," Mads said.

The bell rang. Lunch period was over. Mads and Holly gathered their half-eaten lunches and dumped them into the trash.

"When are you going to talk to Sean?" Mads asked.

"I guess I'll try to catch him before swim practice," Holly said. "Wish me luck."

"Good luck," Mads said. "But if you dump Sean, who will you go to the dance with?"

"I don't know," Holly said.

Sean took the breakup surprisingly well. Maybe it wasn't so surprising. Holly told him she didn't want to see him anymore and she didn't want to go to the dance with him. He looked startled, as if someone had just slapped him. But not too hard. Lightly. He quickly recovered, then looked relieved.

"I'm sorry, Sean," Holly said. "But you know, you really

shouldn't have kissed my best friend."

"She told you about that, huh?" Sean said. "I was hoping that wouldn't get back to you."

"Well, it did," Holly said. "You might want to think about your track record a little bit. Getting dumped by two girls in a row—you're on a losing streak."

"Yeah, that doesn't look good, does it?" Sean said. "What am I doing wrong?"

Holly shrugged. "Maybe we girls are starting to catch on to your game."

"Jeez, I hope not," Sean said. "I've got to go to practice now. Take care of yourself. I'll see you around. And if you change your mind . . . you know where to find me."

"Okay," Holly said.

He went to swim practice. She watched him walk away. Watching him walk—no one could take that from her. When she thought about it, really, his walk was the best part about him. One of the best parts.

"You don't need a date," Lina said. "You can go to the Hap with us."

Holly, Lina, and Mads went to Vineland after school that day to celebrate their détente. Also to work on the Dating Game—they'd been so busy with all the drama, they were behind on posting Missed Connections ads.

They were getting good feedback on it—several couples who met through Missed Connections were going to the Hap together.

"It might feel weird without a date," Holly said. "I don't want to be the fifth wheel."

"You wouldn't be," Mads said. "The girls always dance together, anyway, while the boys just stand around staring at their feet."

"I guess. . . ." Holly said, but she didn't feel very enthusiastic about it. She thought she might just skip the dance this year.

"Holly, did you see this?" Lina asked. "It just came in." She turned her laptop so Holly could read the screen. A Missed Connections ad. "Someone is looking for you."

Mads craned her neck to see. "Ooh, who is it?"

> I want to go to the Hap with the most unattainable girl in school. And that means you, Holly Anderson. Will you do me the honor? I'm good-looking, a sex god, a great dresser and excellent dancer. Reply to me, Locker #534.

"Locker number five-three-four," Holly said. "But that's—"

She looked across the room and saw Sebastiano watching her, laptop open on the table in front of him. He gave her a flirtatious wave.

Holly's locker number was 533. Sebastiano's was right next door.

"I'll be back in a second." Holly crossed the room and sat down at Sebastiano's table.

"Don't make me a four-time loser," he said. "All the other unattainable girls said no."

"I'm aware of that," Holly said. "But for all you know, I'm going to the Hap with Sean."

"I'm well plugged into the grapevine," Sebastiano said. "So I *Hap*pen to know that you're dateless. Since that's a situation that couldn't possibly last long, I thought I'd grab my chance while the window of opportunity was still open a crack."

Holly smiled. He was asking as a friend, of course. She understood that.

"We'll be the coolest couple there," Sebastiano said. "Even cooler than Sean and whoever he scrounges up, assuming he bothers. And we'll be the best-dressed. Especially if you let me advise you on your outfit. You'll look hot!"

"How can I pass up the chance to be dressed by Monsieur Sebastiano?" Holly said.

"Is that a yes?" Sebastiano asked.

Should she? Should she go for the buddy date? It

wouldn't be romantic, but it would be fun. And no butter-flies or complications to worry about.

"Yes," she said.

"You've made me the happiest guy in school," Sebastiano said. The sweet thing was, he meant it.

21 Head Case

In spite of the peace, Mads felt guilty. She'd forced
Holly into another breakup, right before a big
dance. Sure, Holly was happy to go to the dance
with Sebastiano, but it wasn't the same as having a real
date—a real date with the cutest boy in the whole school.
If it hadn't been for Mads and the kiss, Holly would have
gone to the Hap with Sean. She might have dumped him
later, but she'd always have a special memory of that night.

On the other hand . . . now that Holly had broken up with Sean, he was free to ask another girl to the Hap. And Mads was primed to be that girl. The way she figured it, she was first in line. He'd just kissed her, after all! And she knew he liked her; she could feel it. So when would he ask her? What was taking him so long? Every night she lay in bed, wondering *When? When? When?* She couldn't sleep. Her nerves were buzzing.

She'd have to do something about Stephen, of course, once Sean asked her. But until then, she decided to wait. Something told her to be careful and play her cards close to her chest.

To speed things along, she tried to put herself in Sean's path. After school she sat on a bench between the main school building and the swim center, waiting for Sean to pass. The first day she tried this, he didn't walk by. She'd missed him. The next day she went a few minutes earlier. It worked. He was walking right toward her. *Now.*

She pretended to read her biology textbook. She looked up, timing it for when he was only a few steps away and most likely to notice her. He did.

"Hey, kid," he said. "How's the driving going?"

"Great," she said. "Ever since my lesson with you, driving's been excellent. I'm taking the driver's ed test again on Friday. This time I think I'll pass. And it's only my third try."

"Awesome," he said. "And then you'll get your license?"

"No," she said. "I can't get it until my birthday. In August."

"Well, good luck in August," he said, hoisting his backpack over one shoulder. "Later."

"Bye," she said.

He walked down the path. He looked back at her, caught her watching him, smiled, and waved. Then he went into the swim center.

That had been the perfect chance for him to ask her to the dance, and he didn't take it. Mads gritted her teeth in frustration. What was he waiting for? The Hap was next Friday—only a week and a half away. If she was going to go with Sean, she'd need at least a little time to warn Stephen. . . .

The next day, she spent every free period hanging out in the hall near the senior lockers. She even ate her lunch there, sitting on the floor, pretending to be studying.

"What are you doing?" Autumn sat down next to her.

"Nothing," Mads said. "What are *you* doing?"

"Nothing," Autumn said.

"You must be doing something. Your locker's not on this hall."

"*You* must be doing something, too, then," Autumn said. "Your locker's not on this hall, either."

"I'm studying for a Spanish test," Mads said.

"We have a Spanish test?"

"Well, next week," Mads said. "I'm getting a head start."

"I know what you're really doing," Autumn said. "Here he comes."

Sean sauntered down the hall. He stopped and touched the top of Mads' head. She happened to be sitting right in front of his locker. She wished Autumn would go away. What if he was too shy to ask her to the Hap in front of another girl? Though shyness wasn't usually a problem for him.

"Hi, Sean," Autumn said.

"Hi, Sean," Mads said.

"Hi, girls." Sean smiled down at them. He twirled the dial on his combination lock, hinting that he needed to get inside.

"Oh, am I in your way?" Mads asked. "Move over, Autumn."

"You move."

"You both need to move," Sean said.

Mads pushed Autumn, and they slid down a few lockers so Sean could open his. He put some books in and took some books out. He grabbed a couple of pens. Then he slammed his locker shut.

He turned toward the girls. Mads tensed up. Was this the moment? Was he going to ask her now?

"Bye, girls," he said. Then he left.

Mads drooped. Another opportunity lost.

"That was thrilling," Autumn said.

Mads looked at her. "Why are you here, really?"

"I like to watch the seniors," Autumn said. "See if I can pick up any good gossip or fashion tips." She stared after Sean as he turned a corner. "And an occasional Sean sighting doesn't hurt. Kind of perks up my day."

"I know what you mean," Mads said.

"Did you hear he asked Natasha Brearly to the Hap?" Autumn said.

Mads heart stopped. "No! How do you know?"

"It's the kind of thing you hear when you hang out in the senior hall," Autumn said. "That's why I do it."

Mads let the bad news sink in. Natasha Brearly? That witch! Why would he ask *her*? Why not Mads? Why? Why? Why?

What about that beautiful afternoon in the car? The driving lesson? The kiss? Did it all mean nothing to him?

That was impossible. It was the highlight of her life.

It had to have meant a lot to him, too. It *had* to.

Wait. Maybe it wasn't true. "But Natasha has a boyfriend!" Mads said.

"I know," Autumn said. "She dumped him to go to the dance with Sean. Who wouldn't?"

Who wouldn't? Holly wouldn't. But Mads would. And she was an idiot.

"Are you okay, Mads?" Autumn asked. "You look kind of gray. Maybe you'd better go to the nurse's office."

Mads closed her eyes. She felt dizzy. But she knew she wasn't sick. Not in the physical sense. "I'm okay," she said.

She didn't feel okay. She felt crushed, and ashamed of herself, and exhausted.

She'd been willing to sacrifice everything for Sean: her friendship with Holly, Stephen. . . . *How could he ask Natasha Brearly?*

"You're turning kind of whitish now," Autumn said. "It really looks bad."

Mads clutched her stomach. There was that pain in her gut again. Worse than ever.

So he'd kissed her. He kissed lots of girls. She shouldn't have taken it so seriously. She saw that now.

I'm the stupidest, worst person on the face of the Earth, she thought.

"If you're sure you're okay, I'm out of here," Autumn said.

Mads hardly heard her. The pain in her gut subsided. Her strength was slowly returning.

Thank god I made up with Holly, she thought. *Thank god I didn't lose her.*

But what about Stephen? What should she do about him?

She'd been all set to dump him for Sean. It was as if she'd already cheated on him. Would this come between them now, this roller coaster ride with Sean?

Stephen would probably never know about it. But Mads would. Would it settle in the air between them, like an odorless poisonous gas? Undetectable, no color, no smell—but deadly all the same?

22 Kicks

Who's kicking me?" Holly said.

Lina and Mads sat across the lunch table from Holly on Friday afternoon. Lina was nervously jiggling her leg.

"I'm sorry," she said. "It must be me." She held her leg down with one hand to keep it still.

"Ow! Someone is still kicking me," Holly said.

"Sorry," Mads said. "I jiggle my legs when I get nervous."

"So do I," Lina said.

"Well, both of you, stop," Holly said. "What are you so nervous about?"

"My driver's ed test," Mads said.

"Ramona," Lina said.

"Mads, you've got to relax," Holly said. "You tighten up when you're tense. That's when you make mistakes."

"But how can I relax?" Mads said. "My entire life depends on this test!"

"That's not true," Holly said. "It's only driver's ed. I got through it. Lina got through it. We all get through it."

"I wore my new biker boots for luck," Mads said. She lifted one foot to show off her black boots. "And to help me feel cool. Sean said there's no point in driving if you don't look cool."

Holly shook her head. "That is so Sean. It's all about the look."

"You'll pass this time, Mads," Lina said. "I can feel it." She started jiggling a leg again.

"And what about you?" Holly asked. "What's with Ramona?"

"She's asking Rex to the Hap," Lina said. "Right now. I'm waiting for her to come in and tell me what he says."

"Why does that make you nervous?" Mads asked.

"I'm worried what she'll do if he says no," Lina said.

"I'm the one who convinced her to ask him. What if she takes out her misery on me? She'll be impossible to be around. And we're lab partners."

"Here she comes," Holly said.

Ramona sat down at the table. Her expression was grim, but that wasn't unusual for her.

"Well?" Lina said. "Did you ask him?"

"Uh-huh," Ramona said.

"And what did he say?"

"He said no."

"Oh, no," Lina said. Some self-protective instinct made her shield her face.

"Put your hands down, I'm not going to hurt you," Ramona said. "He said no at first."

Lina let her hands drop. "Yeah?"

"But I wasn't about to let him get away with that," Ramona said. "So I said, 'Listen, Bub, you're going to the dance with me, one way or another. Which way will it be? We can do this the easy way, or we can do it the hard way. I'm kind of partial to the hard way myself.'"

"You said that?" Mads said.

"What's the hard way?" Holly asked.

"You don't want to know," Ramona said.

"So then what did he say?" Lina asked.

"He said yes," Ramona said. "He said, 'Yes, Ramona. I

hear you, and I will obey.'"

"He said that?" Mads said.

"Then he kissed my hand," Ramona said. She held out her hand and touched the spot where he'd kissed it. "I think he likes being bossed around."

"He's perfect for you," Holly said.

"You live in a weird universe, Ramona," Mads said.

"No, I don't," Ramona said.

"Yes," Lina said. "You do."

QUIZ: WHO'S THE BOSS IN YOUR RELATIONSHIP?
Circle the answers that are true for you.

1. It's Friday night. You want to go to a concert. Your honey wants to go to a basketball game. You:

   a ▶ flip for it.

   b ▶ compromise: You'll go to the game if you get your way next time.

   c ▶ go your separate ways.

   d ▶ threaten to break up with him if you don't get your way.

   e ▶ do as you're told.

2. Your honey is wearing an ugly shirt. You:

   a ▶ tell him never to wear it in your presence again.

   b ▶ let it pass.

c ▶ give him a new one that you like better.

3. If someone loves you, he or she should make pleasing you his/her first priority.

    True   False

4. Your parents:

    a ▶ always let you have your way.

    b ▶ never let you do what you want.

    c ▶ sometimes let you have your way.

5. Your position in the family is:

    a ▶ oldest or only child

    b ▶ middle child

    c ▶ youngest child

6. When you love someone, his/her opinion of you means everything.

    True   False

7. Your honey hates your friends. You:

    a ▶ dump your friends.

    b ▶ dump your honey.

    c ▶ try to help them all get along.

    d ▶ keep them apart as much as possible.

Scoring:

1. a-2, b-2, c-2, d-3, e-1
2. a-3, b-1, c-2
3. True-3, False-1
4. a-3, b-1, c-2
5. a-3, b-1, c-3
6. True-1, False-3
7. a-1, b-3, c-2, d-1

21-18: You're the boss. You have to have your way. Watch out or you could turn into a tyrant.

17-13: Your relationship is a partnership of equals, mostly. It's healthier that way and likelier to last.

12-7: Your honey is the boss. You like letting others lead. Or maybe you're just a wimp.

23 What's Happening?

You've done very well so far, Madison." Ginny the Gym Teacher sat in the passenger seat of the student driver car. Mads ruled the driver's seat. She glanced at the checklist in Ginny's lap. There was a check next to every part of the test, from proper signaling to three-point turning. Only one part remained: parallel parking.

"One more exercise to go," Ginny said. "But it's a

toughie. For you, anyway."

"I know," Mads said.

She got into parallel parking position. She tried to relax. She looked down at her biker boots. They were cool. She wiggled her toes inside them to let their coolness molecules spread through her body.

She was ready.

She backed into the spot and straightened out. The tires rubbed against the cement. Mads hoped that wasn't a deduction. She pulled forward, which helped a little. She tried to back up. Her tire bumped the curb. She stopped. She was parked. She hadn't totally botched it. Best to leave well enough alone.

Ginny checked her distance from the curb. "You're a little close, but I'll pass you," she said. "Congratulations, Madison." She checked parallel parking off the list.

"Hurray!" Mads wanted to kiss her. Almost.

"Go forth and get your license," Ginny said. "And drive carefully."

"I will."

Mads was floating. She clicked the heels of her boots together and felt a rush of warmth for Sean, in spite of Natasha Brearly. He had really helped her, when no one else could. He was the only person to solve the mystery of parallel parking for her.

She couldn't wait to tell someone the good news. But Sean wasn't the one she wanted to tell. Stephen was.

She ran into the school building, hoping to catch him before he left for the day. She found him on his way out.

"Stephen!" she called. "I passed! I passed driver's ed!"

He grinned and held out his arms for her. "That's great! I knew you could do it," he said.

She jumped into his arms. "I'm so happy! I wish the dance was tonight so we could celebrate."

"We can celebrate anyway," Stephen said. "I'll take you to Harvey's for shakes. And we'll celebrate again next weekend at the dance."

She hugged him tightly. She was so happy she had him. To think how close she'd come to losing him. It was crazy.

"Can I say something?" she asked.

"Please do," he said.

She looked into his eyes. "I can't wait to go to the dance with you. I just wanted to say that, in case it wasn't clear. You're my dream date."

"Me too," he said. "I wouldn't want to go with anyone else."

He hugged her tighter. He looked so happy it almost broke her heart.

• • •

"It's Hap-Hap-Happening!" Sebastiano shouted. He whirled Holly onto the dance floor.

"They are definitely the Happening couple," Lina said to Mads as they watched. Holly looked sultry in a gold strapless fifties dress, her blond hair smoothed and waved over one eye, her mouth a scarlet pout. Sebastiano wore a vintage fifties suit and a shirt flecked with gold to match Holly's dress. They were the best dancers on the floor—thanks mostly to Sebastiano's flair—and looked fantastic.

"Too bad they're not a real couple," Mads said.

Her eyes drifted across the room to Sean and Natasha. They looked good, too, in a different way. Sean had hardly bothered to dress for the dance—but when you looked like him, clothes only got in the way. His one nod to formality was the leather jacket he wore over his jeans and T-shirt. Natasha had put more effort into her outfit, a slinky black dress. The two of them leaned against the wall near the door, as if ready to make a quick getaway.

"I wonder if Natasha's annoyed that Sean didn't dress up," Mads said.

"I wonder if she's annoyed that he can't stop watching Holly," Lina said.

Lina was right—Sean's eyes followed Holly across

the dance floor. Natasha was talking to him, but he didn't seem to be listening.

Maybe he's sorry he didn't try harder with Holly, Mads thought. She wished he was staring at her instead, but he wasn't. She still longed for him, in spite of everything.

Ramona, resplendent in a curve-hugging black Morticia dress, held hands with Rex and watched the dancers from their perch on a windowsill. "I wonder if they'll dance," Lina said. "I've never seen Ramona dance before."

"I can't picture it," Mads said.

"Now you don't have to," Lina said.

The next song was a slow one, and Ramona pulled Rex onto the floor. She put his arms around her waist and danced him around the room in a slow, rocking motion.

Holly and Sebastiano left the floor, shiny with perspiration.

"Slow songs are for suckers," Sebastiano said. "And bad dancers."

"Sebastiano, no more deep dips," Holly said. "I nearly fell out of my dress. It's strapless, you know. As in, nothing holding it up?" She tugged at her gown.

"That's the point," Sebastiano said. "Why do you think dips were invented?"

Sean left Natasha by the door. He walked slowly past Mads and her friends, keeping his eyes on Holly.

"Get over yourself," Holly muttered.

Still, they all watched him. They couldn't help it.

He stepped onto the dance floor, wedged himself between Quintana and her date, and started slow-dancing with her. Natasha looked unhappy.

"I'm glad that's over," Holly said to Mads. "Sean's not the kind of person you can count on. For anything."

"Except parking lessons," Mads said.

"Unlike me," Sebastiano said. "I'm Mr. Reliable."

"I don't know about that," Holly said. "But at least you don't leave me hanging by the door."

Walker and Stephen returned from the drinks table with sodas for Lina and Mads. Stephen whistled their song, "If I Only Had a Brain," and playfully knocked on Mads' head. Then he gave her a kiss.

"Slow dance, my driver girl?" he asked her.

"Let's go." Mads put down her drink and followed Stephen onto the dance floor. He held her in a tender clinch. She knocked lightly on his head. Getting jerked around by Sean made her realize how much she cared about her scarecrow. Not only did he have a brain, but, unlike Sean, he had a heart and courage, too. Knockety-knock.

Does He Like Me?
How Can I Get His Attention?
Is It Normal to Dream About Him ALL the Time?

Love those DATING GAME quizzes? Here's a bonus section just for you!

Check out all the books in the best-selling series by Natalie Standiford, and spend more time with Holly, Lina, and Mads, as they try to sort out their messy love lives with a little bit of luck, lots of pluck, and just the right amount of humor!

BOOK 1: THE DATING GAME

Madison is sure that Sean is the perfect guy for her, but he doesn't know she exists...so she dates his best friend! Lina has a huge crush on her teacher...so she writes him a love poem and submits it to the school's literary journal. Holly is being called "the Boobmeister" by all the guys in school...so she considers paying another girl to parade around in her underwear so everyone will talk about her. Three girls, major guy problems, and a dating Web site—imagine the possibilities!

QUIZ: WHAT COLOR IS YOUR LOVE AURA?

1. To you, a good kiss is:
   a ▶ a peck on the cheek.
   b ▶ lip to lip with a tight pucker.
   c ▶ lip to lip with a little tongue play.
   d ▶ nice and wet with lots of tongue.

2. Your idea of a hot date is:
   a ▶ dinner with your parents.
   b ▶ a stroll and a stop for a cup of coffee.
   c ▶ a movie with an easy-to-follow plot for plenty of makeout action.
   d ▶ getting a motel room.

3. Your favorite pickup line is:
   a ▶ What're you looking at?
   b ▶ Hi. What's your name?
   c ▶ You're cute. What are you doing for the rest of my life?
   d ▶ Shut up and kiss me.

4. You're eating with a guy and he spills ketchup on his shirt. You:
   a ▶ say nothing.
   b ▶ wipe it off with your napkin.
   c ▶ lick it off.
   d ▶ tell him his shirt has ketchup on it, then rip it off.

5. You'll dump a guy if:
   a ▶ he doesn't say "Please" and "Thank you."
   b ▶ he swears too much.
   c ▶ he's got butt zits.
   d ▶ he won't do "everything."

Scoring :
If you picked mostly a's, your love aura is WHITE. Face it, you're a prude. Join a convent now!
If you picked mostly b's, your aura is YELLOW. You're cautious, maybe too much so. Time to take a few chances.

If you picked mostly c's, your aura is BLUE. You're sensuous and sexy but
   don't carry it too far—most of the time. Be careful.
If you picked mostly d's, your aura is RED. You're a total slut! You might
   want to slow down a bit. But hey, maybe it works for you.

BOOK 2: BREAKING UP IS REALLY, REALLY HARD TO DO

Is he "It"? You know—the one-and-only, truly perfect guy?
Suddenly Holly isn't sure that her boyfriend is "It,"—and,
if he isn't "It," maybe it's time to call it quits. Lina is so sure
her teacher Dan is "It," she begins a dangerous e-mail relationship with him that results in a blind date! Madison's "It"
has always been Sean (how could anyone so gorgeous not
be "It"?) until she meets Stephen. Can there be two "It's"?

QUIZ: ARE YOU A DRAMA QUEEN?

Do your friends call you Your Royal Hissy Fit behind your back? Take
this quiz and find out if you're easy-going or a touch too touchy.

1. You break a nail on your way
    to school. You:
    a ▶ don't notice.
    b ▶ stop at a nail salon to fix
        it—homeroom can wait.
    c ▶ sob quietly.
    d ▶ scream bloody murder.

2. Your best friend goes to a
    party without you. You:
    a ▶ hope she had a good time.
    b ▶ resolve to do the same to
        her next time.
    c ▶ sob quietly.
    d ▶ threaten to slit your wrists
        with a nail file.

3. **Your little sister ate the last Oreo (and they're your favorite). You:**
   a ▶ shrug and figure you'll have some another time.
   b ▶ tell on her to your mother.
   c ▶ sob quietly.
   d ▶ take her favorite doll hostage until someone meets your Oreo demands.

4. **You got an F on an exam because you were partying instead of studying. You:**
   a ▶ vow to do better next time.
   b ▶ ask to take a makeup exam.
   c ▶ sob quietly.
   d ▶ threaten to sue the school for discrimination against the handicapped—people with overactive social lives.

5. **You go to a party and another girl is wearing the same dress as you. You:**
   a ▶ laugh it off.
   b ▶ go home and change.
   c ▶ sob quietly.
   d ▶ push her into the pool.

6. **Your boyfriend says he doesn't like the sweater you're wearing. You:**
   a ▶ tell him you like it and that's all that matters.
   b ▶ take it off immediately.
   c ▶ sob quietly.
   d ▶ cut it into tiny pieces and mail it to him covered in fake blood.

Scoring :

If you circled mostly a's, you're a drama peasant, also known as a Cool Customer. Nothing bothers you too much because you've got your priorities straight. Sure, your friends secretly call you an ice queen behind your back, but even that doesn't rile you.

If you circled mostly b's, you're a problem solver. When something goes wrong, you try to fix it—whether it's worth the trouble or not.

If you circled mostly c's, you're a silent sobber. You may not be a Drama Queen, but you've got bigger problems. Consider antidepressants or therapy.

If you circled mostly d's, start the hissy fit now because you're a full-blown drama queen. Congratulations, Your Highness.

BOOK 3: CAN TRUE LOVE SURVIVE HIGH SCHOOL?

Is love forever? Although she's dating Stephen, Madison's eyes keep wandering. Holly gets more than she bargained for when she helps nerdy Britta snag her first boyfriend. And Lina is heartbroken when she accidentally catches Dan and his new love. When the three friends visit Stanford, one thing is clear: the dating game will only get more complicated!

QUIZ: IS IT TRUE LOVE?

It was love at first sight? Or was it?

How can you tell the real thing from a fleeting attraction?

1. When you think of him, you think of:
   a ▸ his face.
   b ▸ his voice.
   c ▸ his body.
   d ▸ the fact that he still owes you five dollars for pizza from the other night.

2. To you he smells like:
   a ▸ fresh bread.
   b ▸ soap.
   c ▸ wet dog.
   d ▸ sauerkraut (and you don't like sauerkraut).

3. When you see him you hear:
   a ▸ a heavenly choir.
   b ▸ violins.
   c ▸ a talk radio station.
   d ▸ fingernails on a chalkboard.

4. On your first date he gave you:
   a ▸ a love poem.
   b ▸ flowers.
   c ▸ nothing.
   d ▸ the flu.

5. Your first words to him were:
   a ▸ "I think I'm in love."
   b ▸ "Nice shirt."
   c ▸ "Is this the line for the bathroom?"
   d ▸ "Move it, Tubby!"

6. **He's like his father because:**
    a ▶ he's honest.
    b ▶ he works hard.
    c ▶ he snores.
    d ▶ he has a pot belly.

7. **Your favorite thing about him is:**
    a ▶ the way he respects you.
    b ▶ the way he listens to you.
    c ▶ the way you look together.
    d ▶ the way he fades into the woodwork when you don't need him.

8. **Your favorite time with him is:**
    a ▶ alone together, kissing.
    b ▶ on the phone, talking late at night.
    c ▶ those funny little silences that prove you don't have to talk to be close.
    d ▶ watching him drive away.

9. **If you had to describe him in one phrase, you'd call him:**
    a ▶ king of men.
    b ▶ nice.
    c ▶ adequate.
    d ▶ scum.

Scoring:

If you chose mostly a's: You've found bliss. True love! Just keep an eye on it so it won't go sour.

If you chose mostly b's: You have a perfectly good relationship. Maybe it will blossom into true love later—you never know.

If you chose mostly c's: You're biding your time with someone who doesn't really grab you. Let go and find someone who makes your heart race.

If you chose mostly d's: Nuff said. You're either cynically using your honey or else you think this is how love should be. Don't settle! And get out of this trap before you turn bitter!

BOOK 4: EX-RATING

The Dating Game has gotten too hot to handle—at least for the school's principal and parents. After Mads, Lina, and Holly come off like sex experts on a local radio interview and their controversial new feature, Ex-rating—where exes rate their former boyfriend/girlfriends—brings in scandalous responses, the Dating Game is banned from the school's computers. But Mads, Lina, and Holly aren't giving up without a fight—even if it means being expelled!

QUIZ: WHAT'S YOUR DATING STYLE?

Are you a Hunter, a Cultivator, a Deer in the Headlights, or Roadkill?

Check all statements that sound like you to find out.

\# ❑ I'm attracted to the cool, quiet type.

@ ❑ I believe in love at first sight.

& ❑ I wait to get to know someone before I will go out with him.

% ❑ I always go after the hottest guy in the room.

\# ❑ I'm shy and self-conscious.

% ❑ I know I'm cute, and I expect the best.

@ ❑ I've been in love with the same person for ages.

% ❑ I have crushes on lots of people at the same time.

& ❑ I believe you should love the one you're with.

@ ❑ I believe there's only one true love for each person on Earth.

& ❑ I like people no one else notices.

\# ❑ People don't notice me.

& ❑ My friends tell me I'm nurturing.

@ ❑ I never seem to like the one who likes me.

& ❑ Nobody's perfect, but I'll find a way to make them better.

% ❑ My way or the highway.

\# ❑ I'm flexible—whatever.

@ ❑ If my guy dumps me, I'll do anything to get him back.

\# ❑ My friends say I'm too hesitant.

% ❑ If I get dumped, I just say, "Next!"

Scoring :
Count the number of times you selected each symbol.
Which one did you pick most? Read that answer section.

%_____ &_____ #_____ @_____

If you chose mostly %s: You're a Hunter. You know what you want and
you're not shy about going after it. Just be careful you don't put some
people off—not everyone likes your sledgehammer technique.

If you chose mostly &s: You're a Cultivator. You're patient, realistic, and most
likely to be happy in love. Just be sure you choose the right person to
spend all that nurturing energy on, or you could find yourself wasting
your time with someone not worthy of your goodness.

If you chose mostly #s: You're a Deer in the Headlights. The whole idea of
love paralyzes you. Maybe you're not ready yet. Or maybe you're just
too insecure. Loosen up and have some fun. If things don't turn out
the way you like, it's not the end of the world.

If you chose mostly @s: You're Roadkill. You think you're unlucky in love, but
we're not talking about luck here, honey. You choose the worst guys,
you approach them in the worst ways, and you leave your heart out in
the street for anyone to cover with tire tracks. Make friends with a
Hunter and ask her to be your mentor. You need help!